I0552387

Grayson's Gift

SILVER SPRINGS SERIES BOOK THREE

KELLI ANN MORGAN

Inspire Books
A Division of Inspire Creative Services
937 West 1350 North, Clinton, Utah 84015, USA

GRAYSON'S GIFT

An Inspire Book published by arrangement with the author

First Inspire Books paperback edition November 2023

ISBN-13: 978-1-939049-66-7
ISBN-10: 1939049660

Printed in the United States of America

"Thank you, by the way," Everly offered. "I'm sorry I didn't say it enough earlier. I don't know what I would have done if you hadn't found me when you did."

"You did thank me. And besides the fact that it is literally my job to make sure no one freezes to death on my watch, I'm glad we met. You intrigue me."

"You're intrigued by women who travel in blizzard conditions with no coat, no food, no phone—that's charged anyway, and no plan?"

He laughed out loud.

"What can I say? I have a type." He handed her the last dish, then reached out to dry his hands on her towel, his fingers brushing up against hers. He took it from her and set it down on the counter along with the newly dried plate.

"Scatterbrained? Impulsive? Unprepared?" she mumbled. She was almost afraid to meet his eyes. If someone had asked her yesterday, those would not have been the qualities she would have used to describe herself, but something in the last twenty-four hours had changed. She couldn't describe it.

"Rare." Grayson's voice commanded her attention, and she raised her gaze to meet his.

"Authentic." He took a step closer, daring her to back away.

"Distinctive." He reached up to brush a strand of hair away from her face and tucked it behind her ear.

"Beautiful." His fingertips lightly grazed the side of her neck, his thumb gently caressing her chin as he pulled her even closer.

Her hands instinctively moved to his waist.

"Grayson." His name spilled from her lips almost as a plea. For what, she was unsure.

PRAISE FOR THE NOVELS OF AMAZON BESTSELLING AUTHOR

KELLI ANN MORGAN

"Strong characters and a compelling story make this an unforgettable trail ride…"

— *RaeAnne Thayne, NYT bestselling author* on THE RANCHER

"This story could have flowed from the pens of the masters; Max Brand, Zane Grey or Louis L'Amour. These greats have stood alone for decades upon an acme seldom reached or yet to be passed by others that have tried. Kelli Ann Morgan has done the unthinkable and written a story that is equal or better than those western-writing icons of the past."

— *Thom Swennes* on THE RANCHER

"I am so excited for the modern branch of the family tree. Morgan really knows how to weave a tale. I love the chemistry."

— *CiCi J* on HOLDEN'S HEART

"Fast-paced romance that'll have you cheering for the characters, while telling them to run at the same time. I love that this series ties in to the other series by Kelli Ann, so you always feel like you're with family."

— *Jenn @ Yeah or Neigh Reviews* on LANDON'S LOVE

"I have never been so emotional in reading as I have with your books. Thank you and keep writing. I'm an 80-year-old cowboy. Again thank you."

— *Amazon Reviewer* on THE IRON HORSEMAN

"A phenomenal read a must-have for any library."

— *Francie* on THE OUTRIDER

"Excellent, well-written plot that kept me reading past bedtime!"

— *Pamela Hastings* on THE WRANGLER

ACKNOWLEDGMENTS

It's been a while, and I am so grateful for all of you who have stuck with me as well as those who help me along the way.

I am so grateful for my copy editor extraordinaire, Rocky, who catches things even when we think we've gotten them all.

I am truly blessed with an incredible team of editors and beta readers—Sarah, Janene, and Ari, thank you for being my go-to gals this time around.

Grant, my alpha reader and love of my life, thank you for always reminding me why I'm a writer in the first place.

I couldn't do any of this without the love and support of my friends, family, and fan-fam. Thank you for waiting patiently and wanting to read my stories in the first place. You ROCK!

To Jenn, Angie, Becky, Susie, Steve,
Tammy, Kenzie, Jill, and Cori...
Thank you for joining me at my table at the
Utah Readers Luncheon this year.
You were a true delight.

Grayson's Gift

SILVER SPRINGS SERIES BOOK THREE

CHAPTER ONE

Silver Falls, Colorado, December, Present Day

"Storm's coming."

Grayson Kane opened one eye and then the other to see the steaming cup of hot cocoa his eldest brother held out for him. He swung his feet down from the porch swing to make room for Holden to sit beside him and breathed in deeply the crisp and invigorating air.

"Yep." Grayson put the mug to his lips but stopped short of taking a drink and glanced over at his brother with squinted eyes. "You didn't put anything weird in this, right?" he asked as he sniffed the hot liquid. "Dirt? Salt? Moldy cheese?"

Holden laughed, extending his legs out in front of him, leaning back, and sticking his hands behind his head, fingers entwined. "Nah. A little nutmeg and cayenne pepper is all—just like you like it."

Satisfied his brother wasn't trying to get him back for putting a sticky note on the bottom of his computer mouse—which had effectively blocked the laser from reading movement and had taken Holden a solid fifteen minutes to discover—he took a sip, reveling in the warmth trailing his insides.

"Thank you."

A storm was coming all right.

A Winter Watch Alert had been dispatched for their area with a blizzard warning. It was nothing new during the holidays in their little mountain town, but one of the new construction companies had closed off the highway to northbound traffic at the exit just before Silver Falls last night. Construction and snow never mixed very well. His officers had already cited several vehicles for speeding, failure to stop, and one accident involving one of Mrs. Harrison's bullheaded Angus cows.

The cow had won. But the old wooden fence had not been so lucky.

"Shelby Miller stopped by last night to see you." The corners of Holden's mouth twitched as he stood up, leaned against the porch pillar, and shoved his hands into his pockets. "She had one of Liv's calendars in tow. My guess is she was looking for Mr. December to sign it."

"Did *you* sign it, *Mr. February*?"

Holden laughed loudly. "Yep. Landon too."

Olivia, Holden's wife, had worked closely with the town book club last year to put together a calendar of Silver Falls' most eligible bachelors to help their brother Landon in his efforts to help those affected by the Silver Mountain Fires get back on their feet. Of course, Holden and Landon were no longer bachelors by the time the calendar was released, but the idea had proven to be very profitable.

"No worries there. Shelby'll find me one way or another. That woman is nothing if not persistent, I'll give her that." Grayson had made the mistake of taking the redhead to the Harvest Festival Dance last fall, and she'd been under the mistaken impression that one date equaled a lifetime commitment. But, for Gray, one date with her had been enough to know that she was not the right one for him.

"You working the late shift tonight?" Holden asked.

Grayson nodded, then took another sip of his hot chocolate. "Can't ask my guys to do what I'm not willing to do myself."

"Up kind of early then, aren't you?"

Grayson savored the last remnants of his cocoa, then stood up. "Nah, I'm still young and spry—unlike like you, old man." He tapped Holden on the arm, a mischievous smile spreading across his face.

Holden raised a brow but said nothing.

"There's a lot to do, big brother. Between getting my chores done around here, gearing up for the festival, and fixing Mrs. Harrison's fence. But don't you worry your pretty little graying head, I'll catch some shuteye this afternoon, so I am ready for, what promises to be, a very busy shift." With a confident nod, he moved to go inside.

Before he could reach the door, Holden materialized behind him, his arm enveloping Grayson's head in a brotherly grip, playfully mussing his hair. "Olivia's got a thing for the distinguished look, you know," he said, his voice tinged with mock indignation.

"Come on, Hold," Grayson called out, half laughing, half protesting as he wiggled against Holden's grip.

The lighthearted tussle carried a sense of nostalgia.

He missed this.

Adulting came with its share of challenges, and with both of his brothers married now, the dynamic of things had changed significantly around the ranch.

After a few moments, Grayson managed to squirm free, surprising even himself, and he slipped backward into a reverse hold with his arms wrapped around Holden from behind, his ceramic cup still clutched in his grip.

Holden, a mix of amusement and competitiveness in his

laugh, seized Gray's arm, leaned forward effectively lifting Grayson off of his feet, and with one hand braced on Grayson's arm, took the mug from his hand and gently set it down on the swing—a silent agreement that their antics were far from over.

In one fluid motion, he flipped Grayson over his shoulder in front of him onto the porch. Grayson scrambled, stretching to gain his brother's pant leg. Upon success, he tugged, bringing Holden down on the porch next to him, limbs entangled and laughter filling the frosty air.

With mutually defeated sighs, they collapsed back against the porch floor.

Grayson took a deep breath. "I've missed this," he voiced aloud his previous thought, his hands resting on his chest.

"Me too, little brother. Me too." Holden smacked him lightly with the back of his hand and sat up.

Grayson followed suit, wrapping his arms around one bent knee.

A few flurries now dotted the landscape.

He loved the ranch. He loved his job. But there was something missing from his life.

Olivia peeked her head out the front door, rubbing her hands over her arms, a quizzical smile on her face and her brow raised.

"What on earth are the two of you doing out here in the cold? On the ground?"

That was it.

A woman.

Holden had found Olivia—or rather, she'd found him. And Landon had Penelope. Even though they all still lived in the main house, their own places were being built further down the road, and it wouldn't be long before it was just him and Granddad. Of course, it was nice to have their parents home for the holidays, but they would be traveling abroad again come spring.

Holden pushed himself up off the porch planks, sauntered over to his wife with an exaggerated swagger, and pulled her into his arms.

"Teaching Grayson who is still the boss around here." The grin that spread across his face made Grayson laugh and he dropped his head in resignation.

"He's got me there."

His brother kissed Olivia quickly before letting her go.

Grayson glanced back out over the yard. Snowflakes barely dusted the earth, but if he didn't get over to Mrs. Harrison's place soon, he'd find himself working to repair her fence in a foot of the white stuff.

A woman?

He scoffed at the thought.

Silver Falls was a small town and, as sheriff, he rarely left. He'd dated half the women in town and the rest were married. It wasn't that he didn't want to settle down, he just hadn't found the person to settle down with. His person.

He picked up the mug from the swing.

"Good morning, sis," he said as he passed her in the doorway with a kiss on her cheek. "You're a good woman to put up with this one." He jutted his chin toward Holden as he stepped past his sister-in-law and headed toward the kitchen.

"Oh, hey, Gray," Olivia called after him. "Rachel McClarin is in town helping her mother with the art walk at the festival and mentioned that they may need an officer or two to help with security."

"Somehow, I don't think any master thieves are looking to abscond with Macy Dawdle's watercolor gnomes, so," he narrowed his eyes, "is this your way of trying to get us to reconnect?"

"Mayyyybe…" She winked. "Just go see her after your shift tonight, okay?"

"I won't be off until after midnight." He knew the excuse would fall on deaf ears. When Olivia got a notion in her head, it didn't change easily.

"I know, but a bunch of them will be at Maggie's place working on some last-minute prep. Be a darlin' and stop by, would ya?"

Her uncharacteristic drawl brought another smile to his lips.

"Of course."

The thought of Rachel McClarin being back in town did put a little spring in his step. The last time he'd seen her, she'd left him with a kiss he'd not soon forget.

A woman. Maybe it isn't such a bad idea after all.

Though he'd have to keep any indication he was entertaining the idea of dating again to himself or he would never hear the end of it. He aimed to steer clear of awkward blind dates and well-meaning set-ups with someone's sister's niece's best friend.

But Rachel.

He could work with that.

CHAPTER TWO

"I hate snow!" Everly Quinn pounded on her steering wheel and squinted against the thickening blizzard as she downshifted into first gear and inched her way up the unfamiliar highway in her old 1975 Ford Courier looking for any sign of civilization.

Everything around her was draped in heavy layers of icing-like white and it had become nearly impossible to see. The brights on her pickup didn't help as they simply illuminated the rushing snow, making it appear like she was in the movies, traveling through space at light speed. It looked cool, but her navigation system was planted firmly in the twentieth century and hadn't yet been calibrated for warp jumps, so she kept her regular beams engaged and her eyes glued as best she could to the road in front of her.

She prayed no woodland creatures would venture out into the night and cross the road in front of her. The voices inside her head kept reminding her that this was the very reason why flights from Albuquerque to Denver had been grounded, and the buses had stopped running at Pueblo.

Too late for common sense now.

She dared a glance over at the box on the passenger seat and shook her head. It was not like her at all to be so spontaneous and foolhardy as to leave the comforts of her downtown city apartment to brave driving through a snowstorm—especially during the holidays. But after the day she'd had, followed by the urgent phone call from her baby sister's husband, how could she have said no? Violet needed her, and now she had no job to keep her from visiting.

She's going to be fine, she told herself. *They are all going to be fine.*

A soft glow appeared in the distance, but as it approached, the headlights detracted from her already compromised visibility. The large pickup roared past her without a seeming thought, spraying a wave of road slush up onto her windshield. Her little truck wobbled from the motion and Everly gripped the wheel even tighter.

Just ahead, the snow blew off one of the signs revealing the mileage for the next few cities. It read…

Silver Falls 7 miles
Allenspark 26 miles
Estes Park 60 miles

Her eight-hour drive had already turned to ten, her phone was nearly out of power, and she'd left her charger at home today, but there were only sixty miles left in her near five-hundred-mile drive. She could do this. If she had been willing to stop anywhere along the way, it would have been back in Georgetown, and she was already well beyond that point.

Everly took a deep breath, pushed the on button to the truck's stereo, and immediately smiled as the music from one of her favorite musical soundtracks came to life and she started to sing along.

I got this.

Flashing lights ahead alerted her that the highway had been closed. An officer stood in the road, diverting traffic on a detour. Again. Lucky for her, there weren't a lot of people out at this hour. She dreamed of her cushy adjustable bed at home and wished she'd taken five minutes to run into her apartment to grab her contoured cooling pillow…among other things. She shook her head again. Impulsive did not become her.

Don't panic, Everly reminded herself as thoughts of her dying phone battery swirled around in her head. Without GPS there was no way she was going to make it to Estes Park tonight.

She pressed the button on the side of her bone-conduction headphones and waited for the beep.

"Call Violet," she said aloud.

Still amazed that her cell phone could follow her commands, the phone rang, and she smiled when her sister's familiar, but tired voice greeted her on the other end.

"Ev, what are you doing up so late?" she asked before Everly could say a word, a slight panic in her voice. "Is everything all right?

"Vi? I should be asking you the same question," she said as she made her way down an unfamiliar roadway in the darkness. "I'm so relieved to hear your voice. Owen called me from your phone earlier and said that you'd been in an accident. Are you all right? Which hospital are you in?" Everly hunched down to peer over her steering wheel as if it might help her night vision.

"No worries, sis," Violet said. "I am fine. The babies are fine. We just walked in the door."

Everly breathed out a sigh of relief.

"Owen was just going to call you. I'm sorry if we worried you."

It was probably not the best idea to be having this conversation with the raging storm waging war on Colorado, but there was something about having someone to talk to that eased the fear she'd been feeling over the last couple of hours as she traversed unfamiliar roads.

"What happened?"

"Let's just say that left turns and lawbreakers don't mix well. Luckily, my boss had the foresight to slam on the gas instead of the brakes. If not, the driver of the other car would have hit my door straight on."

A slight intake of breath on the other end added weight to Everly's foot and she sped up a little despite the storm. She reached out with her heart to imaginarily wrap her arms around her baby sis.

"Sorry, one of the babies has decided to nest in my ribcage. Anyway, the collision snapped the rear axle of his car in half," Violet continued, "spinning us in circles and into oncoming traffic. But a police officer had witnessed the whole thing and had cars diverted away from us in moments."

"Oh, Vi…"

"Then, when I could finally catch my breath enough to get out of the car, the officer noticed my belly—not that it's hard to miss mind you—and he called an ambulance to take me to the hospital. I tried to explain that I was all right, but he insisted. I guess it's protocol."

"I'm so glad he did. You can be quite stubborn when you want to be."

Violet snorted a laugh. "Everly is calling me stubborn." Her voice sounded distant as if she was turned away from the phone. "Owen says it's a Quinn trait shared by both of us."

It was true.

"Fair enough."

Her baby sister's voice grew quiet. "I missed my baby shower."

"What?"

"My friends were throwing me a baby shower tonight, and because the hospital had me and the babies all hooked up to wires and monitoring devices for hours on end…I missed it…" Her voice had become like a piece of music, with crescendos and decrescendos in all the right places to add just the right amount of emotion and drama. "I'm grateful." It was almost a whisper.

That is not what Everly expected Violet to say about missing her own party.

"You're grateful?" she coaxed.

"Yes! What if that accident *had* done something to my babies? What if I lost one of them? Or both?"

In a snap of a second, a blur of black waddled out in front of her little truck and Everly slammed on her brakes, refusing to swerve.

She gasped.

The potential repercussions of swerving had been ingrained in her head after losing a friend that way in high school.

"Everly, are you okay? Where are you?" An insistent Violet asked from the phone.

Luckily, there was not a car following closely behind her, and she glanced out her driver's side window as she now moved at a snail's pace to spot a skunk as it shuffled its way across the snow-filled street.

She exhaled louder than expected, then giggled uneasily.

That was close. She couldn't imagine having to make the rest of the drive with the stench of skunk permeating the air in such close quarters.

Grateful for the technology that allowed her to continue talking to her sister, her hands loosened their white-knuckling grip on the steering wheel.

"Oh, yes. I am fine. Sorry."

The snowfall had grown thick and unyielding as the blizzard raged against the world outside and tormented the archaic vehicle with every violent gust.

Breathe, she reminded herself as her fingers once again tightened unwittingly around the warm leather-wrapped wheel. She reached down to the gear stick, gently depressing the clutch, and downshifted to help the little truck gain some traction.

The road had grown increasingly difficult to see. With no idea where she was, Everly approached a crossroads with three divergent roads. She knew she needed to pull over and try to calibrate her phone's GPS at least enough to have an idea of which direction to go, but there didn't appear to be enough of a shoulder on the side of the road to do that safely.

"Violet, listen, honey," she started, then thought better of what she was going to say. "I love you so much and I am so glad that you and the babies are all right. I'm going to come and see you really soon." She just didn't want to say how soon and add worry on top of tired to her poor sister's shoulders.

"Really? Oh, Ev, I would love that. It's been a hot minute. How long will you be able to stay?"

A hot minute?

It had been more than four years since she'd seen her sister. Of course, not all of that was her fault. The roads moved in both directions. Still, Everly swallowed the guilt.

"I wish I knew—likely a week or two."

"Squee!"

Everly laughed. "I don't think you're actually supposed to say the word, sis."

"When, Ev? When are you coming?" Violet ignored the correction as she pressed.

"Soon."

"I wish you could be here for Christmas," Violet said. "There are so many fun things going on over the next few days—we're heading to this wonderful festival that I know you'd love, but I'll just be happy for you to be here any time of the year. Send me your itinerary and we will come pick you up at the airport. I can't wait to make some fun plans."

Everly smiled despite herself.

"Okay, well, for now, can you put Owen on the phone for me?"

"Okay. Love you, sis!"

"Love you, too."

Rustling sounds in the background filled the silence of the call for a few moments before her brother-in-law spoke.

"Sorry for the false alarm," he said with a sheepish timbre to his voice.

"Owen, don't say anything. Be discreet in your reactions and just listen, okay?" She paused. "Okay?" she prodded again, waiting for his response before continuing.

"Okaaaay," he said with a slight singsong and just the right amount of apprehension.

"I've been on the road all day and am hoping to make it there before morning."

"You what?!?" he asked, alarm evident in the volume and tone in his voice.

"Owen! That is not discreet."

"Sorry. Okay, right, mhmm," he said, his voice suddenly calm and collected as he cleverly masked his initial reaction with an odd sort of laugh. The façade of a smile in his voice was near tangible.

"Better," she said emphatically. "So, I passed Georgetown what feels like hours ago, but this storm is making the travel conditions a little…less than ideal, but now that I know that my sister is all right, I may just pull into a gas station in the next town and try to wait it out." She did not want to tell him that she might be lost.

Beep.

Her phone was dying.

A particularly strong gust of wind made the top of the truck teeter back and forth, and Everly sucked in a breath. She closed her eyes and slowly exhaled through her mouth.

"I don't know if that's wise," Owen said. "I mean," he cleared his throat, "you know your sister. She can't sit still for a minute. She's been nesting like crazy lately, and I might have to sneak her off to that cozy little bed and breakfast in Nederland just to get her to relax. But you're right, it's way too late to travel now, especially with this never-ending snowstorm. It's probably a good thing you're not coming quite yet. The roads are horrible."

Everly was impressed at her brother-in-law's inventive way of telling her to stop in Nederland at a bed and breakfast instead of trying to make it to their place tonight. And he was right. The roads were horrible, and there was no way that staying in the cab of her little truck with blizzard-like conditions would be smart.

"Point taken."

Beep.

She needed to talk faster.

"Traffic has been diverted off the main highway for the third time tonight, but I can see a crossroads ahead. Not sure which direction to take, so I need you to tell..."

All background noise on the phone disappeared.

"Owen?" She glanced at her phone on the bench seat next to her. "Owen?"

It was dead, as was most of her visibility.

"Now what?" She leaned forward, squinting to see the sign at the top of the approaching fork in the road. She turned on her brights. All city names had been obscured from view except one. As she'd never heard of Silver Falls before, she guessed it was probably one of those little Podunk towns with nothing but a gas station grocery store that closed promptly at five p.m. on weekdays and was closed on weekends.

"Nederland it is," she decided aloud but without her phone's GPS, she would have to rely on hope and a prayer to get her to where she needed to go. She glanced from one diverged road to another, then opted to stick to the street that most closely followed the direction of the highway.

With a direction determined, she stepped more firmly on the gas and the engine sputtered.

"What? No! Come on, Herbie, you got this."

The little truck shook.

She knew she should have gone in last week for the oil change that had been on her calendar for months, but her company had just been bought by a bigger fish and new management had had everyone working overtime to catch them up on the entire client database. All expendable appointments had been canceled or rescheduled, but she was beginning to think that truck maintenance should not have been categorized as expendable.

Bright lights appeared, then grew quickly as they approached in the rear-view mirror. Everly squinted, then stomped harder on the gas in an attempt to get out of the way. Herbie jolted forward catching a sheet of ice just as the blare of a horn pierced through the cacophony of the storm and the thunderous roar of an oversized pickup surged past her, leaving a violent wake in its path that sent the smaller truck sliding sideways. She wrestled with the steering wheel, her heart pounding against her ribs as she struggled to regain control of the vehicle before it crashed uncontrollably into a snowbank with a thud.

Gasping for air, Everly released her grip on the wheel. Her neck and shoulders throbbed where her seatbelt had done its job, but as she ran her shaking hands in a patting motion over her head and down her body, she was relieved to find that all-in-all she appeared unhurt.

She was alive. And, for the moment, that was enough.

The shock of the impact left her trembling, but as she closed her eyes and breathed in deeply, counting to eight before exhaling, her nerves calmed, and she attempted to assess her situation. Gravity convinced her that the truck sat at an angled position off the road. Surprisingly, she could still see the moon overhead, though the light reflecting off the snow alone was not enough to see properly, and the interior light overhead had gone out just over a month ago. She reached over and opened her glovebox, fumbling around inside for the small, handheld flashlight she'd won at her work Christmas party last week, and the maps that her father had insisted she keep in the glove compartment tumbled to the floor.

"Just perfect."

She braced herself as she released the seatbelt to gain easier access to the compartment. After a moment of shifting things around, she found it. With a click of a button, the small torch came to life, and she shined it around the small cab. The passenger side of the truck was completely immersed in the snowbank. A push of the driver's side door allowed an unrelenting wisp of bitter cold to thrust its way into the warmth of the truck.

"Curses," she muttered, her voice swallowed by the sudden surge of air and howl of the increasingly fierce wind, so she quickly pulled the door closed again.

Think, Everly. Think.

Surely, someone would stop to help—if they could see her. Thoughts of being buried in the snow without a heater or way to contact anyone clenched at her chest, and she had to force herself to take another breath.

"Let's make a plan," she said aloud, the sound of her own voice providing some small level of comfort.

With a shake of her head and a resigned sigh, she rubbed her arms against the chill. The truck shifted on the unstable snowbank, and her lifeless phone slipped off the bench seat to the floor as if to mock her. She stuck out her tongue at the cheeky device, then bent down to retrieve it, and tapped unsuccessfully on the unresponsive screen.

She certainly couldn't stay in the truck forever—especially not here where she would be more susceptible to having other cars crash into her. Plunged directly into a snowbank at the dead center of a three-way icy crossroad in the near middle of the night with no coat to speak of, no boots, and no phone— the danger of her situation did not escape her.

"Argh…" she let out a disapproving grumble, then tucked the phone into the pocket of her flimsy dress.

A quick look at her gas gauge told her she still had plenty of gas to get her to Nederland as long as she was as close as she believed. If she could just get her truck dislodged from the snowbank, she could get back on the road and find some accommodations for the night. The truck was small. How hard could it be? As she braced herself to open the door once again, her strappy dress sandals became a stark reminder of her complete lack of preparation.

How could she have let this happen?

At least her heater was still working, and she was comforted to know that a fuzzy blanket rested behind the bench seat along with a few other emergency supplies. The truck sputtered again, and she pressed on the gas to give it a little extra oomph, but to no avail.

It died.

"Oh, come on," she grumbled as she turned the keys. The engine grumbled back at her, but wouldn't start up again. Her hands formed a pillow for her forehead at the top of the steering wheel, and she rested her head against it.

"God, please…" she started, closing her eyes, but the rest of the prayer was lost on her lips.

The faint hum of an approaching engine sounded in the distance. Everly raised her head, noting that the intense winds had miraculously subsided for the moment. While the falling snow seemed a little less daunting in the sudden stillness of the storm and from inside the cab of her little truck, it was the red and blue flashing lights reflecting off the wet glass of her window that brought some hope to the otherwise disastrous night.

A patrol vehicle halted in front of her. The door opened and a man, clad in a long sherpa-lined suede coat and a dark Stetson, stepped down. He pulled the collar of his coat closer up around his ears, then, with a flashlight, strode from the back end of her little pickup to the front, seeming to inspect for damage, then came to the window and tapped on the glass.

Everly cranked down the driver's window and peered up at the officer who was kind enough not to shine his flashlight in her face, though his own was shadowed from his large-brimmed hat. When he shifted slightly to the side, the light from his vehicle lit his features and she found herself staring at the most handsome man she had ever seen—and she'd seen her fair share in her industry. The beams accentuated his scruffy, chiseled jawline and illuminated his unusually long eyelashes.

"Seems you've got yourself into a little predicament, ma'am. Are you all right?" His resonant voice, like warm cream in cocoa, was laced with genuine concern.

"I'm stuck," she said sheepishly as she stated the obvious.

"I can see that." He smiled.

Dimples too?

She smiled in return.

"I slid into the snowbank after a giant truck roared past me. My phone is dead, and the truck won't start."

"If you keep trying to start it, you're going to flood the engine. How long have you been out here?"

"Not long," she tried to appear nonchalant, but it was proving difficult with the onslaught of falling snow and the chilling breeze. "Maybe twenty minutes or so." She rubbed her arms.

"Well, I've already called for a tow truck. Don't you worry, ma'am, we'll have you out of that bank and into town before you know it."

"Oh, I don't think we need a tow truck." She was already tired from an exhausting day and the thought of being delayed even more threatened to poke holes in her already waning spirit. "I'm sure if you can just help me get unstuck from the snowbank and give me a jump," her eyes widened, and heat flooded her face, "I mean, if you have cables and could just help me jump the engine, I can be on my way."

"'Fraid not," the man said with a little laugh. "You've got

a flat tire, oil leaking from the undercarriage, and some pretty serious body damage, not to mention a broken headlight and dangling bumper." He pointed at the front of the truck. "That matchbox isn't going anywhere on its own. Not tonight anyway."

Everly's shoulders dropped, and she leaned forward, laying her head against the steering wheel again. "What am I going to do?" she asked under her breath, deflated.

All of the emotion from the day washed over her and tears threatened.

Don't you dare, she warned herself. *This is not the time.*

"We do have one of the best mechanics in eight counties, ma'am," the lawman assured her. "I'm sure he'll get you fixed up before you know it."

She turned her head and looked up at him. Her mechanic back home had already warned her how difficult it was to get parts to keep her little truck in working condition, so she couldn't imagine how long it would take to get them out here—though they couldn't be that far from Denver, so there was hope.

"I'm guessing you're from around here, officer?" Everly asked trying to keep any hint of doubt from her voice. "Silver Falls, I mean?"

"Yes, ma'am. Born and raised."

Of course.

She tapped her head on the steering wheel again, then willed herself to sit up straight, shoulders back, then shivered despite all attempts to be calm, cool, and collected. Another gust of wind whipped through the open window, and Everly couldn't help but rub her arms again against the chill.

At least they grew them well in Silver Falls.

"Is there someone you can call?" the man asked.

Everly scoffed.

"I told you, my phone is dead." Her words came out with a hint of unintended harshness.

"Believe it or not, we do have phones around here. Even in a little old town like Silver Falls. I'm afraid it's hard to get any reception this far outside of town, but you're welcome to use mine once we're in range," he said, a charming glint in his eyes that caused her to crack a smile despite herself.

"Sorry," she mumbled.

"It's quite chilly tonight," he observed, a playful grin on his face. "Nestled up here close to the mountain range, we tend to get a lot more snow than the surrounding areas. This year's been even more than usual. So, with no engine to speak of, you're going to want to put on your coat, wrap in a blanket, and maybe even start a little campfire to keep from freezing out here in that dress that wasn't exactly designed for Colorado winters." He nodded toward her and chuckled.

The baritone timbre in his voice had a calming effect on her nerves and she took a deep breath.

"A campfire?"

Just how small was this town?

"Yeah, let's skip the campfire for now," he suggested with a wink, sending a gentle tingle down her spine. "The tow truck'll take another twenty minutes or so to get here."

How could she tell him she didn't have a coat or even a change of clothes to speak of? What did she have that could help keep her warm?

Besides him?

The thought surprised her—mostly.

Everly Quinn, you stop that right now.

"I've got a blanket behind my seat," she blurted without thinking. "I'm sure that will take off the chill until then. Would you mind giving me a hand with the door? I can't get to it from here."

The officer opened the door and instinctively moved to hold it open, then held out a hand to help her up. She glanced from his face to his extended hand, then slipped hers inside. The moment her feet touched the ground, it was like she'd become a reindeer on roller skates, and she fell like a klutz into his broad chest. He caught her up against him, his arms wrapped around her for support.

So cliché, Everly. So. Cliché.

But as she looked up to thank him, she didn't care. It felt good to be in a man's arms again, a good-looking man's arms—even if it was by accident.

CHAPTER THREE

"Whoa," Grayson's arms shot out, snatching the wide-eyed beauty around the waist as she lost her footing on the slush and ice beneath her feet.

She reached out, but her attempts to steady herself were to no avail. She fell hard against him, clinging to his arms as she struggled to regain her balance. Yet, the unforgiving ground did little to assist, particularly given her fancy, open-toed, high-heeled sandals.

A medley of intoxicating scents mingling honeysuckle and ripe peaches, enveloped her, piquing his interest further. He stood his ground as her grip tightened on his arms, and finally, with one well-timed step, she was able to stand. Without letting go of him, she looked up, her wide eyes framed by lightly smudged lashes, and suddenly the idea of letting her go felt far less appealing. He couldn't help the smile that formed on his lips as their eyes locked.

"Is it just me, or did we just skip a few steps in the getting-to-know-each-other dance?" he asked, then immediately regretted the cheesy line.

She breathed a laugh, and he swore that even in the semi-darkness he could see fresh color tint her cheeks. He liked it. It had been a long time since he'd been so intrigued by a woman.

The snow had already begun to accumulate in her hair and if the temperatures continued to drop, she would be frozen before Gertrude arrived with her beast of a truck. From what he'd seen, the woman didn't have any luggage to speak of, so he wondered what she could possibly be doing out in a blizzard at this time of night in a compact pickup barely suited for damp roads, let alone a full-blown snowstorm.

"Thank you," she whispered, a touch of embarrassment in her voice as she attempted to take a step backward, then squealed as one foot went awry and she clutched onto him even tighter.

Instinctively, Grayson pulled her in a little closer, appreciating the excuse to hold her a moment longer.

She reached up and tucked a loose strand of hair behind her ear and bit her lip before looking up at him again. "I'm not usually so...awkward." Flakes now danced with her lashes, and she started to shiver.

Grayson normally dreaded construction in the winter—especially when it diverted the main road traffic off the highway and onto his smaller roads. While the state's budget allowed for plenty of salt, production vehicles, and an abundance of manpower to keep the roads clear, small towns like Silver Falls had to rely on one or two small companies and a handful of volunteers using plows on the fronts of their pickups to plow the back roads in, out, and around town. Tonight, the lack of resources had brought him his fair share of work, but one look at the beautiful woman stranded in the snowbank, and he'd known she was going to be trouble.

Unable to tear his gaze away from hers, he glanced down at her lightly pouted lips and resisted the urge to kiss her.

Settle down there, Kane. You just met the woman.

He reasoned that his recent thoughts about finding someone to share his life with had been occupying his mind more than he'd care to admit, and now, he wondered if he was merely projecting his desires onto this moment, causing him to see a connection that didn't exist. Although, his granddad had always told him there were no coincidences, just untapped opportunities.

Maybe he'd get the chance to find out.

"Excuse me, ma'am," he said, clearing his throat and dropping his hands to her hips only long enough to guide her out of the way. He reached past her into the cab of the small truck and lowered the seat to retrieve the blanket she had mentioned stashing there.

When he turned to face her again, holding up the thin, fringed throw she believed would provide some warmth, he realized they were still standing remarkably close to one another. She hadn't moved a step. He fixed his gaze on hers as he leaned forward, manually rolling up the driver's side crank window.

The woman accepted the blanket from him, wrapping it somewhat haphazardly around her shoulders.

"You must be new around here," he said as he stood up to his full height. "I've yet to have the pleasure. I thought I knew everybody from Silver Falls." Grayson had taken note of the New Mexico license plate when he'd done a quick assessment of her vehicle, but it was hard to fathom her traveling so lightly if she didn't live nearby. He'd certainly never seen her before. She'd be hard to forget.

"Are you staying with someone in town?"

"No. I'm not from around here, but I'm headed to Estes Park to spend the holidays with my sister and her husband."

"That's still quite a distance from here. Especially in this weather."

"I know."

"Well, you're certainly not going to make it there tonight. Let's get you into town to see if we can find you someplace to stay." He knew the inn was probably full—especially on such a stormy night just days before the festival, but he had to get her in out of the cold.

"Can you just drop me…off…at the bus station.n.n.n…and I'll come back…later to pick up my truck?" Her teeth had begun to chatter, she was visibly shaking.

A short burst of wind caught the fringe on the edge of her throw and blew it upward, knocking one corner from her hand and inflating the skirt of her dress.

"You are going to catch your death out here," he chided, unfastening the buttons of his coat with precision. "The way I see it, ma'am," he continued, a note of concern lending an edge to his voice, "you've got two choices. Either you can crawl back onto that tilted, soaked bench seat of your freezing-cold cab while you wait for the tow truck, or,…" he shrugged off his coat, bracing himself against the sudden chill, and draped it swiftly around her shoulders. He rubbed his hands briskly up and down her arms. "Or, you can come with me and wait inside my truck where the heater is most certainly working, and the seats are dry and warm." He gestured over to the Bronco.

An icy gust swept over them carrying a thick trail of snow. Visibility was diminishing quickly, and the hollow bursts of wind seemed to mute all other sounds.

"That," she said simply, though Grayson could barely hear her over the storm. "Let's do…that."

He didn't waste another moment, already feeling the flakes melting through his shirt, puckering his skin from the cold. He tucked an arm around her, kicked the Courier door shut, and covered her head with her worthless little blanket as he led her to the passenger side of his truck. He helped her up, wishing he hadn't already drained the hot cocoa from his thermos.

"I'm Everly, by the way," she said with a weary smile before he shut the door. "From Albuquerque."

"Sheriff Grayson Kane, ma'am." He dipped his head, water dripping from the brim of his hat. "Welcome to Silver Falls."

CHAPTER FOUR

Warm air enveloped Everly as she stepped through the open door to the inn that the sheriff held for her. She shook off the chill that followed and pulled the man's coat more tightly around her. Timeless holiday classics greeted them, immediately providing the Snowy Pines Inn with a cozy, traditional feeling. It wasn't too surprising to see someone standing behind the desk of the small bed and breakfast at this hour, but she had certainly not expected to see so many people in the lobby. Fresh scents of pine and cinnamon greeted her in waves as she noted several tables full of evergreen boughs, pinecones, sprigs of holly, and ribbon.

Visions of the last Christmas they'd had together as a family before her mom left, crept into her mind, and she half expected to see roasting sticks and marshmallows sitting on the hearth of the fireplace and reams of paper with scissors lying out on the table for making snowflakes to decorate the tree.

The door closed loudly, and people turned their heads to look at them.

"Well, speak of the devil." An older woman, adorned in

jeans and a cream-colored flounce-sleeved blouse, smiled as she made her way toward them. She greeted the sheriff with a quick hug and kiss on his cheek.

"You talkin' about me, Mama?" Grayson asked with a sly grin as he took off his hat and ran a hand through his hair. "Good things I hope."

Everly could see the resemblance between the two.

"The ladies were just asking me if I preferred one month out of the year over another." She winked at Everly and breathed out a laugh.

Odd question. Seasons, yes, Everly definitely had a favorite season, but month?

"Well, aren't you going to introduce me to your friend here, son?"

"Of course, Mama. I found her crashed into a snowbank on the side of the road."

"Oh, no. Are you all right, dear? Are you hurt?" the sheriff's mother asked, placing her hands gently on Everly's shoulders and peering at her with a furrowed brow. The woman's genuine warmth and concern touched her.

"Hello." Everly raised her hand in a wave and giggled when she realized her fingertips were barely visible above the shearling coat's sleeve. "I'm Crashed-in-the-Snow Banks, but my friends and family call me Everly. Quinn."

"From Albuquerque," the sheriff chimed in.

"And thanks to your son, I am not going to freeze to death out in this storm."

"Well, Miss Banks—uh, I mean Everly Quinn," the woman corrected with an amused grin. "From Albuquerque," she added as she glanced back at her son. "You must be exhausted and near frozen through in those clothes." She wrapped an arm around Everly and pulled her into a little half hug before guiding her over toward the plush couch in front of the fireplace.

The sheriff had cranked up the heat on the way to the inn,

and despite having to walk the forty feet or so through the snow to the entrance, the icy grip in her bones had begun to relent, and she was feeling quite human again.

"Why don't we just sit over here by the fire," the woman continued, "and my son will get you something warm to drink." She glanced up at Sheriff Kane who nodded and strode over to the other end of the room where a copper drink dispenser, stacked ceramic mugs, and what looked to be several pumped flavorings and fixings graced a refreshment table.

With the merging of companies at work, Everly had been heading into the office earlier than ever to assist with the integration for the past few weeks—pouring over client files, rechecking every box for upcoming events, and modifying themes and concepts for new marketing campaigns. While it had taken a toll on her sleep habits and social life, she'd believed the investment would pay off. The sacrifice of being out the door and to work by five each morning had earned her nothing more than a cleared-out office and her things packed into a wooden box.

When they reached the fireplace, Grayson's mom sat down on the wooden coffee table and motioned for Everly to sit on the couch across from her.

Resigned and too tired to resist, she tucked her legs up beneath her and leaned onto the arm of the couch. "The sheriff told me you are all up late working on Christmas decorations for a community Christmas festival that begins this weekend."

"That's right. Most of us here are on the festival committee this year. Every year, we swear we will get the decorations done early, and every year here we are two days before it begins stringing holly berries on pine boughs and gluing pinecones to candles." She laughed. "If the weather keeps up like this, there may not be a festival to speak of. This blizzard was certainly not in the plans, but it looks like it arrived at precisely the right time, and perhaps with a touch of serendipity, hmmm?"

Everly glanced over at Grayson, unable to keep a soft smile from turning up the corners of her mouth.

It had been a long day, and now, her tired eyes burned with need for sleep. She was ready for bed and was afraid that if she sat on this overly comfortable couch for too long she might just fall asleep.

"What can I do to help?" Everly asked as she glanced around at the others working at the tables. "I haven't done Christmas decorations in a long time, but I'm generally pretty good with my hands." Her philosophy was that it was always better to be busy than bored—not that tired and bored were the same thing, but until she had a decent place to lay her head, she felt like she should be doing something.

"Nonsense. You can rest for a bit. I'm sure there will be plenty of time to help later. How long do you think you will stay here in Silver Falls, Ms. Quinn?"

"That's a good question. My sister lives with her husband in Estes Park. I was on my way to surprise her for Christmas when that truck pushed me off the road. I should call them and let them know I'm okay. Depending on the weather, I'm sure Owen would be happy to come pick me up tomorrow."

"So soon?"

"Honestly, spontaneity has never exactly been one of my strong suits. I usually have my days planned out down to the nanosecond. This whole trip is a little uncharacteristic for me, but I'm sure I'll feel back to myself after a good night's rest. Things will be more clear in the morning."

As they spoke of rest, Everly's body gradually surrendered to the inviting embrace of the crackling fire. She nestled into the corner of the couch surrounded by the heavenly scents and sounds of Christmas. Her elbow rested on the cushioned arm, and she idly twirled the stray tendril of hair at her temple.

"Thank you for this, Mrs. Kane. After the day I've had, I

needed a little time to just sit and relax."

"Call me Cass, please." She crossed her legs and leaned forward, her elbow on one knee. "He likes you, you know."

"What? Who?"

"Grayson is my youngest. Funny, kindhearted, dedicated. Handsome too, don't you think?"

"Very," she said without hesitation, then thought better of it and smiled sheepishly at the man's mother.

Cass smiled back knowingly.

Overly tired did not look pretty on Everly and her tendency to say anything that came to mind when she needed sleep didn't generally help in any given situation.

"All three of my boys are good-looking men if I do say so myself," Cass said with an appreciative bob of her head. "They take after their daddy. And mine." She smiled again and Everly could see that she was a proud mama. "In fact," she continued, "they were all selected to be models for a charity calendar that just came out for this upcoming year."

"Thus, the question about your favorite month." Everly nodded, now understanding the question she'd overheard when they'd first arrived.

"Exactly."

"But I thought Grayson was the sheriff."

"Oh, he is, dear. Holden's an architect and Landon a photographer."

"Not models?"

Cass shook her head.

"But they all posed for the same calendar?"

"Yes, ma'am. You see, my daughter-in-law—who is an amazing romance novelist by the way—selected and convinced twelve of the most eligible men in Silver Falls to participate in the calendar because it was for a good cause. Shelby over there has a copy if you'd like to see it."

"I would love to see it. Though, I must tell you, Cass. I think Grayson takes after his mother. He definitely has your cheekbones."

Her face flushed with color at her praise.

"And his father's dimples," she added.

Oh, those dimples.

Everly unwittingly glanced over at the sheriff. A woman in a beige cashmere v-neck sweater and navy pencil skirt walked up behind him, running her hand across his back and resting it on his shoulder as she leaned up against him.

A pit dropped in Everly's gut. She'd not stopped long enough to consider that the sheriff might be dating someone. Or worse, married. She groaned inwardly. So, why had Cass made a point of talking him up?

Sleep deprivation and stress had begun to play tricks on her, conjuring imaginary scenarios in her head. He'd caught her when she slipped. Gave her his coat when she was cold. Yes, there had been no definitive actions or words indicating he shared the same connection she felt. However, there was one fleeting moment out by the truck where he had held her in his arms just long enough that as he'd gazed down at her, it seemed as though his eyes had briefly wandered to her lips, and for a heartbeat, she'd believed he might kiss her.

Silly girl. Of course, he wasn't going to kiss you. He doesn't even know you.

He's the sheriff, an obvious protector. He'd been friendly. Nothing more. Still, the inexplicable disappointment caught her off guard and she returned her focus to his mother.

"He *is* single," Cass said simply as if reading her thoughts.

Heat flooded Everly's face at the idea she'd been caught watching him. By his mother no less. It wasn't like she was sticking around this little town for long enough for him to be anything more than a distraction. Though, still, the thought pleased her.

Single.

"Maybe someone should tell her." Everly's eyes widened, and she slapped her hand over her mouth. She needed sleep.

Her filter had already gone to bed.

Cass laughed. "Oh, there's history there all right, but Rachel left town a long time ago. Left *him* a long time ago." She lowered her eyes as if remembering something from years long past.

"She's here now." Everly couldn't help but feel the slight sting of jealousy.

What did it matter? Grayson was handsome and charming, but she lived in Albuquerque. Had a life there. At least she'd had a life there. There was certainly a lot to consider over the holidays.

"We'll see for how long." Cass raised a brow. "She's only visiting her mother for Christmas, and then she'll be off again in the new year."

"One hot caramel apple cider, check." Grayson appeared, holding out a steaming mug with a swirl of whipped cream boasting from the rim sprinkled with flecks of cinnamon.

A man's voice called out from one of the tables, "Cass, I need your opinion on something. Can you come over here for a minute?"

"If you'll excuse me, my dear." The older woman patted her on the knee. "Duty calls."

"Here," the sheriff said as he sat down in the same seat his mother had just vacated. "It will warm you from the inside out." He removed his hat and set it down on the coffee table next to him. His hair fell in a swoop in front of his eyes, and he pushed it back.

"Thank you," she said, meeting his eyes in the light for the first time.

The warmth from the mug in her palms soothed her and she leaned in to savor the delightful aroma wafting from the cup.

Grayson chuckled.

"I have cream on my face, don't I?" she asked, quickly sweeping the bottom of her nose with the back of her fingers.

"Not quite," he said, extending his hand toward her. "Here." His thumb gently brushed across her cheek.

"Are you always so…charming?" she asked, reveling in the sensation of his warm hand on her face.

"You think I'm charming?" He raised a brow, a warm smile and mischievous twinkle appeared as he slowly lowered his hands into his lap.

Everly bit her lip as she looked up at him, unsure whether or not the heady warmth rising in her face had come from the fire or the cocoa or from something entirely different.

"Grayson?" Cass returned, heaving a large box full of books and toys. "These gifts need to be wrapped for Santa to put under the Christmas tree for the children. Will you take them home and make sure they get that way?"

"Yes, ma'am. I'll take care of it," he replied, taking the box from his mother.

"Is he for real?" Everly asked.

She couldn't think of a single man who'd been in her life who would have been so willing and eager to help wrap gifts for anyone, not even the big guy himself.

Did I just ask that? Out loud?

Must. Have. Sleep!

Cass laughed loudly.

The chittering of conversation halted momentarily throughout the room and several people stopped what they were working on and looked over at them. She just smiled broadly and waved. "I think the newcomer is a bit impressed with our sheriff," she called out to them.

Everly bit her lip sheepishly, heat increasing in her cheeks.

With several nods and smiles, it wasn't long before the group had returned to their tasks.

"What did I do now?" Grayson asked innocently, feigning a shrug.

"Don't be so modest, Gray." The woman in the cashmere sweater appeared from behind him. "If anyone is the embodiment of the Christmas season," she directed her comments to Everly, "it's Grayson Kane." She smiled warmly. "Hello. I'm Rachel," she said, her hand remaining on the sheriff's arm.

Everly so had not wanted to like the woman, but it was hard not to like someone who was so dynamic and generous with her praise. She seemed sincere enough.

"Everly." She nodded.

"Oh, I assure you," Cass started, "as handsome as he is,…"

Grayson grinned wide and winked dramatically, raising his eyebrows and nodding.

Cass smacked him playfully on the arm.

"…my son has his faults. But he is nothing if not sincere."

Everly could swear that a little color now stained the man's cheeks.

"Well, it has indeed been such a pleasure meeting you, Miss Everly Quinn from Albuquerque. Now, I must go help Ethel finish those garlands and add the finishing touches to the lanterns or we'll be here all night. I'm afraid I might fall asleep on my feet. I'll bring that…thing," she winked, "…over for you to see tomorrow."

The calendar, Everly reminded herself.

Grayson narrowed his eyes. "Why do I get a feeling you two are up to something?"

"Up to something? Heaven's no," Everly replied. "I just have to know your recipe." She held up her mug. "Actually," she said, slipping her legs out from beneath her and sitting up straight, "do you mind if I help?" She slapped her free hand on her knee and used it as a springboard to help her stand. "I'm afraid if I sit here much longer, I might fall asleep too. I would love to help. Really."

Cass met her eyes and looked at her hard for a good, long moment.

"While I appreciate your generosity, Everly of

Albuquerque, by your own words you've had quite a day and I imagine that you must be exhausted," she said with a knowing smile as she placed a hand on Everly's shoulder. "We're almost finished here, dear, but if you're up for it tomorrow, Grayson will need some help wrapping those gifts, and I do have three giant wreaths that still need decorating. I would love any help I can get."

"Of course."

"I could help too, Mrs. Kane," Rachel piped in.

"Oh, no you can't," a woman called from across the room. "We will be pricing all the art pieces, wrapping them, and taking them down to the City Center Gazebo to find the best places to hang them."

Rachel heaved an acquiescent sigh. "Mom's right. There are so many pieces. It's going to be a lot of work." She turned to the sheriff. "Maybe you could come and help tomorrow, Gray?" she asked, her eyes wide, brow raised, and an endearing smile pouted just enough.

Everly attempted to smooth her own straggly curls, knowing she must look a sight in comparison, and she wanted to hate Rachel more than ever for looking so perfectly quaffed at this late hour.

"Maybe you could come too, Everly?"

Really? That was unexpected. *She's so…nice. Definitely can't hate her. Dang it.*

"I don't…" Everly shook her head slowly, forcing a smile, but her energy was waning.

Grayson lifted the big box of toys a little higher. "I'm afraid we're going to be a little busy tomorrow, Rach, wrapping presents and decorating *giant* wreaths," his emphasis on the giant part earned him scrunched eyes and pursed lips from his mother. He smiled, and a hint of laughter touched his voice. "I will, however, talk to the guys about getting some extra security to walk the streets during the art walk."

What have I gotten myself into? At this rate, she would never get to Estes Park in time for the holiday.

"Thank you," Rachel said with only a hint of disappointment in her voice. "I'm sure we'll figure something out. We always do."

"Okay, let's stop all this lallygagging and let Everly get up to her room for some rest before we put her to work tomorrow. You are staying here at the Snowy Pines Inn, aren't you, dear?"

Everly glanced over at Grayson.

He shook his head.

"No room," he said with a shrug. "I just spoke with Hugh, and he told me they are overflowing through Christmas day. The festival always brings a crowd, but this year the promise of Eli Thomas is making everyone a little crazy."

Eli? Here?

Everly didn't know what to process first—the fact that there literally was no room in the inn at Christmas and she was stranded alone in this little town in the middle of the night during a blizzard, or the fact that her past was catching up to her faster than she could imagine.

"Wait, let's back up the truck a little," she spilled out the familiar phrase her father had used a thousand times over growing up. "Did you say that Eli Thomas…Eli Thomas, the too big and handsome for his own britches fantasy young adult writer Eli Thomas is coming to Silver Falls? Here…in this town…for this little festival of yours?"

"One and the same. The dreamy, wealthy, and now writing a Christmas children's book set in Silver Falls Eli Thomas."

"Can we please stop saying Eli Thomas?" Grayson rolled his eyes, then looked at her. "Don't tell me that you are a fan of his too."

"Oh, I won't. Nope. Not a fan." Everly turned to Rachel, curiosity getting the better of her. "He's writing a children's book?"

"Yes. Eli is an old friend of mine from college. I may have told him a thing or two about growing up here, and now he decided to write about a small-town Christmas using Silver Falls as the backdrop."

Everly nodded and smiled a smile she did not feel. "I have to go." She started for the door, then stopped short.

Where was she going to go?

Nederland. But obviously not tonight.

She could not be in Silver Falls when Eli arrived. Would not.

"Hey, Albuquerque, where do you think you're going?"

Everly dropped her head and snorted a little laugh.

"I'm sure I can find another hotel or something close by. It's just for the night. I'll just rent a car or catch a bus up to Estes Park tomorrow." Luckily, she'd been stashing away money in her savings account for a rainy day and it couldn't get much rainier than this.

Or snowier.

"Well, then I guess it's settled," Cass said loudly.

"What's settled?" Grayson asked. "The closest hotel that might have a vacancy right now is up in Nederland and it's after midnight."

"She'll go home with you."

Midnight?

She'd totally lost track of time. Owen and Violet would be worried sick.

Wait. Go home with the sheriff? Her heart skipped a beat or two.

"Can I borrow a phone?" she asked, walking back to where Cass, Grayson, and Rachel all stood staring at her.

"I'm not going to let you go back out in this weather. Besides, you'd be hard-pressed to find someone crazy enough to pick up fares at this time of night in a storm."

Let me?

She raised a brow.

"Why, Sheriff, are you worried about me?"

"It's my job."

Well, that was true.

She should explain.

"I was talking to my brother-in-law when my phone died. I don't want them to wonder if I'm dead in a ditch somewhere. I'd just like to let my sister know that I'm all right. So,…may I borrow your phone?"

"You can use mine," Rachel said, turning on her heel and rushing over to the table at the far edge of the room.

Grayson set the big box of gifts down near the front desk and reached into his back pocket.

"What's her number?"

"Why, so I can let the 'sheriff,'" she raised her arms and made air quotes, "call them and give them a heart attack? I don't think so."

His expression grew serious.

"I'm sorry." He shook his head. "That is not what I meant," he said, meeting her eyes with a mixture of warmth and gravity as he handed her his device. She handed him the mug of cider she still held.

"Good news," Rachel said, returning with her phone in hand. "Dad just told me that the manager over at the Hillside Motel across town just called back and said they've had a vacancy in one of their rooms."

"Nonsense," Cass chided. "She'll go home with Grayson."

"I'll do what?"

"Wait, what? I don't think—"

"We've got plenty of room in the barn, and several of the rooms are still made up from Olivia's reader retreat. It's just perfect." Cass stepped forward, placed a knowing hand on Everly's arm, and smiled. "Grayson will drive you, dear. To Silver Springs Ranch."

To sleep in the barn?

CHAPTER FIVE

Grayson could not take his eyes off the ill-clad beauty as she spoke animatedly on his phone. Exhausted, hair in disarray, and freezing, Everly had managed to hold it together— had even retained a splash of humor. He liked her. And he liked how she looked wearing his coat.

"Will you get her set up out in the main bedroom behind the studio, love?" his mother asked. "I think it will be quite well suited to our guest, don't you think?"

"Yes, ma'am," he said, collecting his hat from the coffee table and setting it atop his head.

"Good man. Now, if you'll excuse me. I'd also like to get home at some point tonight. My bed is calling my name."

"That snow isn't going to let up for long, Mama. Are you sure you don't want to come home with us in the Bronco?"

"Oh, no, darling. Your dad is over there helping Hugh untangle the twinkly lights for the gazebo. He brought the snowcoach. We'll be fine and we'll see that the others are too—right after we finish up here, but you need to get that girl a place to sleep, and the barn is as good a place as any." She winked.

"Yes, ma'am," he said again, this time with a chuckle. Dad had requisitioned a four-seat snowmobile for traveling in conditions like this. It combined the comfort of an enclosed dune buggy with the efficiency of a snowcat. It was still a prototype, but was not lacking in test runs.

"I think I'm going to call it a night too," Rachel said. "It's been so lovely to see you, Gray." She stood up on her toes and kissed him on the cheek. "Talk tomorrow?"

"Sure."

"Thank you so much for that," Everly said, clearing her throat as if she might be interrupting something. She handed his phone back to him, her eyes darting back and forth between him and Rachel.

He was keenly aware that the latter still held his arm.

"Um," Everly bobbed her head, suddenly appearing a bit flustered. "Owen said they had been, um, about to call the police," she rocked back and forth, nervously tucking a piece of hair behind her ear, "so it was, uh, a good thing that I called when I did."

Grayson shrugged. "Dispatch would likely have put the call through to me as I was the sheriff on duty, but I'm glad they didn't have to worry any longer than necessary."

"Right, well, it has been very nice to meet you, Everly," Rachel said. "I hope you have a safe trip home tomorrow." She nodded, slid her hands down his arm, and squeezed before letting him go. "Goodnight."

"Goodnight." Everly waved and offered the woman a genuine smile. "By the way, Rachel," she said, "you have impeccable taste. That's a beautiful sweater."

Color flooded Rachel's face and a little sparkle appeared in her eye. She was obviously pleased by the comment.

"You have a good eye. It's a Sophia Reynaud," Rachel told her.

It took everything in his power not to roll his eyes at her unexpectedly pretentious response. Did anyone know who or what a Sophia Reynaud was?

Just take the compliment, woman. Say, thank you!

With one last wave, Rachel headed down the hall. The McClarin's had owned the inn for as long as he could remember, and they never rented out her room.

Grayson paused for a moment to appreciate that just this morning he had been lamenting the absence of a woman in his life. So, admittedly, when he'd found out Rachel was back in town and wanted to see him, he'd been naturally a little curious to follow up on their last encounter and see if there was anything to it.

Everyone had believed that she'd broken his heart when she'd taken a job so far away, but the truth was, they'd always just been good friends. The way she'd kissed him the night she left had been anything but friendly and had planted a seed of possibility in his mind, but now, after having met Everly, he knew he could never feel the same for Rachel.

"Will I be heading home tomorrow? Or to Estes Park at least?" she asked hopefully.

The more selfish part of him hoped that he would at least have a few more days to get to know her.

"I suppose that will depend on this weather, and how long it will take Frank to fix your…"

"Truck?" A knowing smile touched her lips.

He coughed.

"Yep."

Looking down at the mug in his hands, Grayson realized it had grown quite cold while she'd been on the phone. He set it down on one of the tall, round tables that had been set out for collecting guests' snack dishes, then grabbed Everly's hand and pulled her over to the table with the big copper kettle dispenser.

"Trust me, it's better hot." Grateful they still had some insulated to-go cups, he quickly made up a single-serving size batch of his recipe—cider an inch and a half from the rim, two

pumps of caramel, a splash of cinnamon flavoring, and a
dollop of whipped cream sprinkled with fresh ground
cinnamon.

Delicious.

He topped the cup with a domed travel lid and handed it
to her, smiling when she held it with both hands and
scrunched in her shoulders as if it would provide warmth to
her entire body.

"This is very kind, thank you."

The moment the liquid touched her mouth, she closed her
eyes, an audible groan escaping her lips.

He chuckled quietly, pleased at her reaction.

"Good?" he asked.

"Heavenly." Her eyes fluttered open, and she met his gaze
with a smile. "I don't mean to rush you, but can we go home
now? I mean go to your home. Where I am going to sleep. In a
retreat room—whatever that means." She breathed out a
flustered sigh. "Can we leave?"

"Yes." He laughed. She was clearly exhausted, and
Grayson felt terrible that he'd kept her here so long. With one
hand, he swept across the air in front of him, inviting her to go
ahead. "Goodnight, everyone," he said as he picked up the box
of toys near the entrance.

A small chorus of voices called back. "'Night, you two."

Twinkling lights from the eaves of the quaint little
building danced with large flakes of snow falling and swirling
around them as Grayson and Everly left the warmth of the
cozy inn. While the storm had let up some, Grayson knew all
too well how quickly things could change in the midst of a
snowstorm, and he wasn't convinced this one was done. He
pulled the front door closed and smiled to himself at the sing-
song sound of the jingle bells Hugh had installed to notify him
when a guest had arrived.

Enough snow had accumulated just since they had arrived
to completely obscure the two short stairs to the front porch

and hide all evidence that there were any visitors inside the inn. Everly pulled the shearling coat up closer around her ears, her shoulders scrunched, and she held onto her cup of hot apple cider as if it were a lifeline.

"Wait here," he told her as he tromped down the path to the truck and set the box of gifts inside. He started the engine and turned on the heated seats.

While the McClarins ran and lived in the Snowy Pines Inn, several other committee members would be leaving soon. Grayson had told the committee members many times over the years they should avoid these late nights as much as possible, but they were a determined bunch and against his advisement, had decided to get together and finish their festival preparations even in the midst of the storm. It gave him some level of comfort to know his dad had brought their snowcoach and could see some of the others home.

"I'm just going to quickly shovel the walk. Would you like to go back inside and wait for a bit?" he asked. He strode past her to grab the snow shovel from behind the porch rockers.

She lightly tapped the snow on the top stair with her foot, attempting to test its depth.

"If it's all the same to you, I think I'll wait in the truck."

"I wouldn't—"

Before he could stop her, Everly took the step down, then let out a light squeal when it was farther down than she'd expected and wavered, once again attempting to gain solid ground.

What was it with this woman and thinking she could traverse the icy path in her sandals like they were heavily treaded boots?

Grayson lunged forward to catch her from falling face-first into the snow. He grasped the back of the sherpa collar on his coat and tugged her backward a little too hard. Her arms flailed about as she tried to regain her balance, the back of her hand smacking into his nose with sickening accuracy,

and the hot cider she held dropped beside him on the snow-
covered porch, miraculously landing topside up. He gripped
the coat tighter despite the pain now emanating from his face
and the tears forming in his eyes, determined not to let her go,
but her feet gave way as she slipped right out of his coat and
slid down the snowy steps onto the ground like a sled on her
backside.

Grayson shook his head and stretched his face against the
warmth collecting near the bridge of his nose.

"Everly, are you hurt?" he asked, making it to her side in a
jump and a stride. He held out a hand to help her up, ignoring
the throbbing in his face and blinking away the tears that still
plagued his eyes.

She looked at his hand, then at him.

"Does my ppppride count?" she asked through chattering
teeth as she took his hand, brushing the snow off the front and
back of her dress with her other hand. "How…did I ever let
you convince me…to leave the couch next to the fire?"

"I guess you didn't want to wait? Or go back inside for
five minutes?"

"It's really cold out here," she said, shivering without the
protection of his coat.

"Exactly." He shook the snow from the coat, but as he
went to put it around her, her body jerked, visibly shaking.

"Okay, up we go. And no more mishaps with those
impractical shoes of yours," he said matter-of-factly as he
swooped her up into his arms. She was a little more substantial
than she looked and that only endeared her to him more. He
tromped through the snow to the truck, opened the door, and
set her inside on the passenger seat. "Let's get you warmed
up."

"These seats are already warm," she stated with
incredulity. "How are they already warm? I mean, I know *how*
they are already warm, I just have never actually experienced
it." She placed her hands beneath her thighs directly on the

seats.

"I guess your little matchbox wouldn't have come equipped with heated seats," he teased as he shook the snow powder off his coat and opened it so the inside sherpa would be up against her skin as he wrapped his coat around the front of her.

"I assure you, Sheriff, I am not normally the damsel-in-distress type." Her lips quivered, her hair dripped, and she pulled his coat up to her chin.

"Excuse me," he said, leaning in toward her. He reached into the backseat and retrieved her blanket from the floor. "I don't know about a damsel-in-distress, but I do know you could use some sleep." He placed the blanket over her legs. "Now, wait here," he directed again. "I am just going to shovel the walk, and then I'll get you home."

Her head bobbed like one of those wobbling dolls.

Grayson made quick work of clearing the path up to the house and the stairs. With a generous sprinkle of the ice melt that Hugh always kept in the garden box next to the porch, he was satisfied that the trek out to their vehicles would be a safer one for his parents and other committee members.

He looked up into the sky.

"At least until it gears up again," he said aloud.

If it wasn't for the freezing and fatigued woman in his truck, he would have been tempted to offer a police escort home to all of them.

The drive back to the ranch was uneventful and quiet. When he pulled up onto the road in front of the barn, he glanced over at Everly who leaned against the passenger door, asleep. He almost hated to wake her.

His phone chimed. He pulled it from the cupholder where he'd stashed it when he'd gotten in and quickly glanced over the text his mother had sent him. She'd already called and spoken with Olivia, and she and Penelope had turned down a room and set out some anticipated needs for their first non-retreat guest.

"Good," he whispered. They had all called it a night and were already on their way home.

It was nice to have his parents home for the holidays—even if it was only until the new year. They'd barely made it home in time for Holdon's wedding, had been here to watch Grayson walk Penelope down the aisle when she and Landon were married, and had made this year a priority to be home for more than a week at Christmas. While they worked abroad, they had plenty of opportunities to travel all over the world. It was their philosophy that it was better to do it now while their knees still worked than trying to do it after they retired.

"I'm not sleeping," Everly said groggily, her voice a little deeper than it had been just half an hour ago, her eyes still closed. "I just don't know if I can get my body to move. Are we there yet?" She snorted. "I sound like I'm six years old on a road trip."

With a chuckle, Grayson turned off the truck. "We're here."

Snow flurries had turned into giant snowflakes, and they now came down at increasing speeds and thickness.

"Let's get you inside." He jumped out of the truck, tucked his chin closer to his chest, and ran around the vehicle. Everly sucked in a surprised breath the moment he opened the door as snow blew in swirls all around them.

Grayson half expected her to whine about the cold and take her own sweet time getting moving. But, to his surprise, she tore off her seatbelt and jumped down from the truck, raising her hands above her head and using his coat as a makeshift umbrella.

Her first step on the snow in those heels nearly landed her back on the ground, but Grayson slipped his arm around her and lifted in a sort of half-carry. He only let go of her for a moment once they reached the barn doors so he could pull them open.

"You are not seriously going to make me sleep in a stable, are you?" she asked. "At Christmas?"

He detected a slight hint of amusement in her voice and chuckled, glad that even as tired as she was she hadn't lost her sense of humor.

Once inside, he closed the doors and reached for the lights. He remembered to turn on only the first and the last switch to create the ambient feel.

"Wow," Everly said, draping his coat back over her shoulders.

Olivia, his romance-writing sister-in-law, had just completed her third author-reader retreat, but this was the first Christmas event in the newly renovated barn. His eldest brother, Holden, was an architect and had gone all out in his design of the bed-and-breakfast-style barn—complete with a full kitchen and six bedrooms, a recreation and craft room, and several little 'reading nooks' as Olivia called them.

A welcoming wash of warm air greeted them as they stepped inside. A fire roared in the hearth. Big, round, cream-colored string lights glowed from the rafters, the sixteen-foot Christmas tree was illuminated with twinkling lights amidst rustic jingle bells and red bulb ornaments, and the garland above the fireplace was decked out with poinsettia blooms and even more lights.

They'd been expected.

Thanks, Mama.

"This is unlike any barn I have ever seen." Everly glanced around the room with awe.

Warmth spread from deep in Grayson's belly as he watched the wonder dance in Everly's weary, but beautiful eyes. He saw the room again with a new perspective. A neutral gradient-shaded plush rug accented the matte-brown, heated concrete floors which were the perfect backdrop for the red bows, rustic jingle bells, and twinkling lights adorning the tree. He had to admit, the barn had far surpassed his expectations as well. Up to this point, he had only seen the place during the day while he was helping out with the retreat, but to experience it at night was a whole other story.

While it had certainly made the impression he was sure Olivia had hoped for, Everly appeared to be blinking in slow motion.

She's fading.

"Come on," Grayson said, unwittingly grasping her hand and guiding her down the hallway to the bedroom behind the office that his mother had specified. "There should be a clean pair of pajamas laid out on the bed and fresh toiletries in the bathroom." He pointed to the small door just to the left of the open bedroom. "And you'll find extra blankets, should you need them, in the closet there.

"I don't know what to say."

"How about, 'goodnight.'" He smiled and tugged lightly on the brim of his hat.

"Goodnight, Sheriff." Everly handed Grayson back his coat and leaned up against the doorframe as if it were the only thing stopping her from falling over. "Thank you."

As she closed the bedroom door behind her, he smiled to himself.

"Untapped opportunities."

CHAPTER SIX

Light peeked into the room, reaching beneath Everly's eyelids to bring attention to the fact that it was indeed morning. She opened her eyes slowly, then closed them again. She was still dreaming, she was sure of it. The savory aroma of bacon cooking wafted beneath her nostrils and a soft glow of light bathed her face in warmth, and she snuggled a little deeper into the thick, down comforter that engulfed her with its significant weight. A smile graced her lips as the face of one Sheriff Grayson Kane skipped through her mind and, for a moment, she had no care in the world.

She was warm.

She was rested.

She was safe.

It had been a long time since she'd slept so well, and she made a mental note to ask Grayson where they'd gotten these pillows. For years she'd tried one promising pillow after another until her bed was nearly overflowing. With a little shake of her shoulders and nestling her head back into the perfect combination of fluff, firmness, cooling memory material, and softness she flipped onto her back and draped her arms on the outside of the blanket.

After several moments of luxuriating, she willed herself to sit up. Refreshed for the first time in what felt like ages, she glanced around the room with new light. A decorated Christmas tree sat in the corner of the room next to the white fireplace with a wooden mantle decorated with lighted garland. Two French doors, adorned on the edges with sheer, white curtains, opened out to her own personal snow-covered veranda. And that view…mountains, pine trees, and snow as far as she could see. Light flakes still tumbled down to the ground. It was almost like she was encased in a snow globe, secluded from the rest of the world.

A low rumble of machinery was quickly followed by sounds of animals coming to life outside. A gentle lowing of what Everly guessed were cows, clucking chickens, and the nickering, neighing, or whinnying sounds—she knew the terms but had no idea the differentiation between them—of horses met her ears.

She was, after all, on a ranch in the middle of nowhere, Colorado. She imagined that the storm probably brought a lot of additional work for the people here.

"I should probably call Vi." She glanced at the nightstand. Her phone was not there, and she strained to remember what she had done with it last night but couldn't place it.

With an exaggerated exhale, complete with puffed cheeks and rounded lips, she was impressed that the red and black plaid blanket that had been folded into a strip still lay undisturbed across the foot of the bed. She must have been out last night like a light. Normally, she awoke to her blankets in complete disarray from tossing one way and another all night long. She tilted her head and sat up straight, realizing that a pair of Christmassy pajamas had indeed been laid out for her and now sat on the corner of the bed. Everly glanced down at herself and vaguely remembered crawling under the covers without any consideration of changing her clothes.

Without another thought, she scooped the outfit with one hand, then threw the blankets off of her legs and swung them over the edge, hesitant to step down onto what promised to be cold concrete floors. She braced herself for a moment, then jumped out of the bed, only to be pleasantly surprised that the floor beneath her feet was warm.

Heated floors? Are you kidding me?

Who were these people?

When she took her first step, she kicked something soft and looked down to find a pair of fuzzy slippers sitting just beneath the bed. She giggled and slipped her feet into them, laughing at the ears that protruded from the front and the little pompom at the back. A bear maybe, or a snow bunny she guessed.

"Where did Grayson say the bathroom was?" she asked aloud, then remembered it was just to the left of the bedroom.

She opened the bedroom door slowly and peeked her head out into the hall. The smells that greeted her caused a little rumble in her tummy and she realized she hadn't eaten since yesterday afternoon when she stopped at a drive-through in Santa Fe for a bite.

As Grayson had told her, a brand-new toothbrush sat on the countertop as well as a packet of make-up remover wipes, a travel-size deodorant, mini toothpaste, a new hairbrush, and a tube of mascara and chapstick. All things to make a woman feel human.

"A woman after my own heart," she said, smiling that there were women at the ranch. Mascara and lip balm were a lifeline to most women who also wanted to look refreshed and awake.

The pajamas looked like something she could lounge around in all day. Yoga pants and an adorable top—heather grey front that read, 'This is my Christmas movie-watching shirt,' with a picture of an old-fashioned red truck hauling Christmas trees, and buffalo-check three-quarter length sleeves. Honestly, anything would be better than the flimsy little dress she'd worn to work yesterday.

The realization of everything that had happened just in the last twenty-four hours struck her, and she sat down on the closed toilet seat, toothbrush in her mouth, and just breathed.

Everything is going to work out, Ev. It always does.

The more she tried to convince herself of that, the harder it was to believe.

Though, she thought as she looked around, *this place is incredible.*

Even the bathroom had a touch of the holiday spirit with its decorative towels and chai soap. When Everly finally emerged with a fresh face, brushed hair, and more comfortable clothes, she felt like a new woman. She returned to her room, draped her dress over the stuffed chair near the window, threw the covers back into place on the bed—knowing she could never make it look quite as fancy as it had been when she arrived—then, she followed the Christmas music playing softly overhead into the festive living space. She was again amazed that a barn could possibly look like this on the interior. It was even nicer than that chalet they had stayed in on location last year in Grindelwald for work.

Her eyes were immediately drawn to the bookcase at the far end of the enormous fireplace near the front of the room. A toasty fire was already aglow. All she needed was a cozy sweater, a cup of hot peppermint cocoa with marshmallows, and a good book to curl up with on that fluffy, plush, cream couch, and she would be in heaven. As she perused the bookcase, she discovered that a few thrillers and mysteries adorned the shelves, but a good majority of the books were romance, particularly Olivia Blake novels. Everly scanned through them until she found what she was looking for.

Christmas at Blackwood Ranch.

"A bit on the nose for me this Christmas," she said with a little laugh as she pulled the book from the shelf and hugged it close to her chest before turning it over to read the description. Even though it had been out for a couple of months, she'd not yet had a chance to sit down to read the latest Blackwood novel.

"I hear Logan Blackwood is even dreamier than Bentley."

Everly nearly jumped out of her skin. She hadn't heard anyone enter the room, and she looked over to see a beautiful blond woman, whose hair dangled in pig-tail braids, wearing only a bit of mascara and lip balm for makeup.

She smiled, shaking her head lightly, and held up the book.

"I've actually always preferred Aidan myself," she said, her smile broadening at the thought of the youngest Blackwood brother. "You must be the brilliant woman who lent me this outfit and provided me with fresh toiletries in the bathroom. Thank you! It's a horrible feeling to know you literally have nothing but the clothes on your back—especially as ill-suited as they were. These are so soft and comfortable."

"I'm glad they are to your liking. We weren't sure about sizes, but they look great on you."

Everly beamed under the woman's praise. "We?"

"I'm Olivia, or Liv if you prefer. And Penelope, my sister-in-law, should be here anytime now." The woman stepped forward and pulled her into a light hug. "Welcome to Silver Springs, Everly. It looks like you are going to be staying with us for a few days?"

"Oh, I wish I could. This place is absolutely amazing. It's been a long time since I've been somewhere that actually made me *want* to celebrate Christmas. But I was hoping to spend the holidays with my sister. I know my truck won't be fixed for a while, but I was thinking I could catch a bus or get a car to take me up to Estes Park today. It's only an hour or so from here, isn't it?"

"Oh, honey, I hate to be the bearer of bad news," Olivia said, "but I'm afraid you're stuck with us. At least for the time being. With this storm, tractors, snowmobiles, and sleighs are about the only vehicles that are able to get around right now. You'll be hard-pressed to even get into town, let alone anywhere outside of it. There are road closures everywhere. One of the joys of living in the mountains."

Everly took in the information. It helped to know that her sister was all right after her accident, and now, the fact that she didn't have a job to get back to seemed a momentary blessing.

"For how long?" She wanted to prepare herself. Not having a plan was so far out of her comfort zone that she again chastised herself for not thinking things through before she left.

"Well, that depends entirely on how long it takes for this storm to let up." Olivia glanced out the window, then put her arm around Everly's shoulders. "Why don't you come on into the kitchen and have something to eat? I've made some crepes, bacon, and fresh squeezed orange juice."

Everly's stomach grumbled again. "You made crepes?"

"Come on. Grayson left a note for you on the counter. He and the boys are out delivering hay to the cows and making sure these drifts haven't blocked their water sources. I expect them back within the hour."

As they headed into the kitchen, Everly spotted the box of gifts from last night sitting on the floor next to the couch.

"What about the festival?"

Olivia laughed. "If there is one thing I have learned about Silver Falls, if it's important to them, they will find a way. They always do."

Everly didn't see how they would be able to do anything out in this weather. It was beautiful, but she couldn't imagine having to spend the entire day out in it. She sat down on a barstool in front of the island. Her phone sat next to a little folded notecard with her name on it.

Hey, Albuquerque, I thought you might
want to call your sister and let her know we're

snowed in for at least twenty-four hours, so I
went ahead and charged your phone. After we
take care of our chores, I'll be back with tape
and wrapping paper. Make yourself comfortable
and relax until then. —G

"Seriously, is he for real?" she asked Olivia, holding up the note.

The woman laughed. "The Kanes are a rare breed, that's for sure. I'm guessing it's the Redbourne in them. Just wait 'til you meet their granddad. Ian likes to think of himself as the living and breathing Theodore Blackwood."

"He reads Oliv-i-a Blake...novels." She glanced over at the woman spooning custard onto a crepe and narrowed her eyes before widening them. "Oh, my goodness, I can't believe I didn't put it together before. You...are Olivia Blake. This," she held up the novel she'd placed on the counter, "Olivia Blake?"

"Olivia Kane," the woman corrected. "But, yes, those are my novels. I wrote them, at least. Those particular books belong in Ian's collection." She beamed at Everly. "I'm just thrilled that you like them."

"Like them? I love them!" She eyed Olivia. "I have so many questions."

The barn doors scraped open and the sounds from outside grew louder momentarily.

"It smells divine in here," a female voice called out.

Moments later, another woman walked into the kitchen decked out in a gorgeous fur-lined, large hooded parka cinched at the waist with fur-trimmed sleeves. She looked like someone out of the movies. She set a very expensive-looking camera down onto the countertop, took off the coat and laid it over the back of one of the barstools, then draped an arm around Everly's shoulders.

"Is this her?" she asked Olivia. "The woman who's put a

little spring in our handsome little brother's step? And charmed our highly selective mother-in-law in mere minutes?"

"One and the same."

Everly felt the heat creep into her cheeks and didn't quite know how to respond. "I don't know about all that, but I am the one who is super grateful to be inside your beautiful home, safe and warm."

"Oh, this isn't where we live—though, isn't it absolutely extraordinary all decked out like this for Christmas? It's Olivia's pet project. We live up at the main house and outbuildings. At least until our own homesteads are finished up the road." Penelope popped a berry into her mouth.

Main house?

"What she means," Olivia said, handing Everly a plate with a beautifully plated crepe complete with whipped cream and berries, "is that I have a lot of hair-brained ideas and a husband who likes to indulge my every whim."

"How would that be?" Everly muttered more to herself than anything.

"It is true about Holden, he sure loves to spoil her, but don't let her fool you. She has a head for business and big plans for this place." Penelope reached down to the cupboard on the side of the island and retrieved a laptop. Within minutes she had loaded pictures from her camera onto the computer.

"Are you a photographer? Professionally, I mean?" Everly asked.

Olivia snorted. "Pen is not only a professional photographer, and cover designer extraordinaire," she smiled endearingly at her sister-in-law, "but she and Landon have been invited to showcase their work in the Lens and Light Exhibition at the The Grand Gallery in the Hudson Art Center in Santa Fe next month."

Everly perked up at the sound of something familiar. "One of my dearest friends has a few paintings on display in the Hudson Art Center. I've been there several times. It's only an hour or so from home."

"And, where is home?" Penelope asked.

"Albuquerque. At least, for the moment."

Olivia leaned down with her elbow on the counter, her chin resting on her fist, and Penelope closed her laptop and turned, both staring at her.

"For the moment? There is definitely a story in there," Olivia said with a raised brow and a coaxing smile.

"Not really. I just don't really have a job to get back to anymore is all. I have a lot of thinking to do to figure out what's next for me."

They continued to stare, heads bobbing slightly as if to encourage more information.

"Boyfriend?" Penelope asked.

"No."

"Family?"

"One sister."

"Parents? Grandparents?"

"Nope. Just me and Violet."

Olivia nodded her understanding. "What was the job you don't have to get back to anymore?"

Questions were coming at her faster than she had expected, and she had to stop and think for a second. "I was the Creative Director of Client Relations for R&J Media—it's an event coordination and media/client relations company." The short description had been practiced many times to simplify the complexities of her job when talking to media outlets.

Olivia raised a brow.

"And you quit?"

"I'm afraid that is a story for another time." Everly shifted uncomfortably in her seat. She didn't want to talk about her job—didn't want to even think about yesterday's mishap—and needed to redirect the conversation. "Who is Landon, by the way?" Everly hoped the question would be enough to distract

them from asking any more questions about the mess of her
life back home.

"He would be my husband." Penelope raised a finger in
the air. "Holden," she nodded at Olivia, "is the oldest Kane
brother, then Landon, and Grayson is the baby."

"Okay, I have to ask," Everly said as she cut into her
crepe. "Are they all as charming as the sheriff?"

In unison, both of the women said, "No." Then laughed.

"At least not initially," Penelope added.

"Don't get me wrong," Olivia said, "Holden is sexy and
thoughtful, but it took a bit to break through his exterior.
Charming is not the word I would have used for him when we
first met. He wasn't too excited to see me when he'd learned
his granddad had invited a romance novelist to hold a retreat at
Silver Springs." She chuckled. "He'd hated the idea."

"And Landon," Penelope started, "well, he's a little more
reserved and perceptive, but his talent is beyond compare and
he is the most loving and complimentary man I've ever met. A
little bold when he needs to be, but let's face it, I really like that
about him. And he has this look that just melts me from the
inside. And his voice…"

"Okay, we get it," Olivia said playfully, "you are in love
with the man."

"Is it that obvious?"

Why was it so easy to talk to these women she'd only just
met?

"And Grayson?" Everly asked, her tone even as she
attempted to downplay her interest in the man.

"Oh, I don't know, what can we say about our little
Grayson?" Olivia rolled custard into another crepe.

Everly almost choked at the word, 'little.' From her
perspective, he was anything but.

"Well, he's personable and fun-loving," Penelope said
thoughtfully.

"Handsome and helpful," Olivia added as if they were

checking off items on a list.

"A protector who would give anyone the shirt right off his back," Penelope said.

"Quite literally," Everly chimed in, unable to stop the smile that twitched at the corners of her mouth. "Last night, he actually gave me the coat right off his back in the middle of a storm because I didn't have mine." She shivered just thinking about what she would have done had he not come along. "I guess it's just hard for me to believe there are still men like that still out there. Sincere and chivalrous. That has not been my experience—especially from law enforcement."

"I knew it," Olivia said. "There's a story there. And you like him."

"What's not to like?" There was no use in denying it. "He's very good-looking. And *charming*," she emphasized the last word, aware she'd already used it before. "He's respectful of his mother, makes a mean hot caramel cider, loves Christmas. And he's…I don't know…playful, strong…" she held up her fully charged phone, "…considerate."

She'd only known the man for all of ten hours but was amazed at what she had learned about him in that time, and there definitely had been some spark between them.

"But?" Penelope coaxed.

"But…it's complicated."

If they only knew…

"Oh, honey…it always is," Olivia said, pouring some fresh orange juice into a small glass over ice and pushing it toward her.

How could Everly share with them how every man she'd ever allowed into her life had let her down in one way or another? How her fiancé had left her at the proverbial altar just days before the wedding when his publicist, and her colleague, convinced him that being married would hurt his image and his bottom line? How her father had constantly chosen his job as a police officer over his family—a decision that had ultimately gotten him killed in the line of duty? Or how she had gotten fired from her job of five years because she rejected the new boss's advances?

Men in her world didn't open doors for women. They didn't wrap Christmas gifts or shovel sidewalks. And they certainly didn't provide beautiful accommodations for stranded women without any expectations. If Grayson Kane was for real, he was truly extraordinary.

"So, what's wrong with him?" She couldn't help herself from asking. She brought the glass up to her lips and then peered over the rim at the woman who'd poured it.

"Well, the man can't sit still. He's always on the move." Penelope was quick to answer.

"He over-commits himself to helping others—especially those less fortunate or elderly," Olivia piped in.

Both women thought for a moment.

"Oh, what about his constant need to improve every aspect of his life," Olivia offered. "He's always taking one class or another. Would you believe he has taken up pebble art? Pebble art of all things. He seriously goes on walks and picks up pebbles off the ground to make pictures or collages in his off-time—not that he has much of that being sheriff and his duties helping out around the ranch."

"What about his tendency to take his work home with him?" Penelope winked at her, and they all laughed.

Everly couldn't deny the connection there had been between them.

"Okay, I get it," she chuckled breathily, "Grayson has the kind of faults that aren't actually faults at all. I've been on the hiring end of interviews when people play off some of their strengths as weaknesses. Don't think I don't see what the two of you are doing. But if he is as wonderful as he seems, why isn't he taken?" Thoughts of the sheriff did strange things to Everly's insides, but she hadn't been looking for a man or a relationship. Eli left a little over a year ago, and she wasn't sure she was ready to jump head-first into something new—not that that is what they were insinuating.

"If I didn't know any better, I would think the two of you were playing matchmaker."

Penelope conveniently took a sip of the drink Olivia had just poured for her.

"I'm flattered, ladies, truly. What girl wouldn't dream of being set up with a man her favorite romance novelist deems a worthy catch? But you don't even know me. I could be some psychotic stalker, an insipid mooch, or worse, a totally self-absorbed narcissist."

"Are you?" Penelope asked, leaning against her shoulder.

"Of course, not. But would I tell you if I was?"

"Good point." The woman to her side picked up a slice of bacon from the plate in the center of the island and slipped it into her mouth.

"Call it a gut feeling," Olivia said with a fleeting glance at her sister-in-law. She cut into her own crepe. "Besides, it takes a lot to win over Cassandra Kane, and you managed to do it in less than ten minutes. That is saying something." She pointed her full fork at Everly. "And…to be perfectly honest, we may have done a little research about you online," the last part rushing like spring run-off before she shoved her fork into her mouth and smiled.

Everly racked her brain to think about what information they would have found about her online. Unfortunately, dating a celebrity had come with a few minor inconveniences, and having much of her life put on display had been one of them.

She closed her eyes and dropped her head.

Her breakup had been more public than she would have liked, but she'd walked away fairly unscathed as the masses had been more focused on the newly eligible writer than on the woman he'd discarded.

"Eli Thomas was an idiot. *Is* an idiot," Olivia consoled. "My publisher said he's too big for his own britches, and that he'd let go of the best thing that ever happened to him."

Everly looked up at the woman, her brows scrunched.

"How?" She shook her head. "Who?—"

"Ryan Blevins," she provided before Everly could finish her query. "She thinks very highly of you, by the way."

Small circles.

"When?—"

Stop with the one-word questions, Everly. You sound like a dolt.

When would they have had the time to do any research on her? Had they stayed up all night? And when had they possibly had the time to talk with Olivia's publisher?

"Research is one of my superpowers." It was as if she could read her mind too.

Everly glanced back and forth between the two beautiful women, sat up a little straighter in her chair, and spoke calmly and in a full sentence. "It's hard not to feel a little intimidated here."

"Whatever for? You, my dear, are a great catch. I think—"

Penelope cleared her throat.

"*We* think," Olivia corrected, "that you and Grayson are perfectly suited for each other."

"Did I hear my name?"

CHAPTER SEVEN

A tingling sensation surged from Everly's heart at the sound of the sheriff's voice. She pushed her shoulders back, folded her lips together to freshen her balm, and unconsciously ran her hands over her hair.

"You like him, like him," Olivia accused playfully and with delight in a tone barely above a whisper.

Everly didn't know why she was so nervous. She had interacted just fine with plenty of men in the past whom she'd thought attractive, so why did her chest feel like it had been inflated with air and dozens of tiny little butterflies had suddenly hatched from their cocoons and were flying about?

"Morning, ladies," Grayson said as he strode into the kitchen, "my ears are burning something fierce. All good things, I hope."

"I hear you have a tendency to bring your work home with you," Everly forced her pounding heart to calm.

"Only when it's worthy of my time," he said, locking eyes with hers and smiling. "Albuquerque," he said in acknowledgment before popping a piece of bacon into his mouth, "I trust you slept well." He leaned down onto the island in front of her, his arms extended, one fist cupped in his other hand, his face now level with hers.

The catchlights in his eyes reflected the warm glow of the fire and they seemed to change colors from hazel to gray.

Olivia and Penelope exchanged glances and knowing smiles.

"I did," Everly affirmed, bobbing her head slowly. "I did," she repeated. "Great actually. The room was just the right amount of cool. The blankets were like sleeping in the midst of weighted clouds. And I have to ask, where in the world did you all get those pillows? I felt both supported and comfortable. All. Night."

They all laughed in unison.

"No, you don't understand. That is unheard of for me. I must get one."

Penelope gasped. "Oh, no. Is that really the time? I have got to get these photos processed," Penelope said, pushing her chair back and putting her closed laptop into a purple bag. "Is Landon up at the house?" she asked Grayson.

"He grabbed his camera and headed back out to the north pasture to capture the Belgians. Since the wind has died down, it seems they are actually enjoying playing in the snow. It's still coming down pretty good out there, so I expect he'll be back shortly." He moved to stand up. "Would you like me to give you a ride up to the house?"

"It's like a hundred feet. Is it coming down that much?"

"I'd just hate for that precious laptop and camera of yours to get wet."

"You bring a sled?"

"Yes, ma'am."

Penelope put her elegant coat back on, draped her laptop bag over her head and shoulder, followed suit with her camera bag, and then held out her empty hand.

Grayson pulled the keys from his pocket and gave them to her.

"Sit, Gray," Olivia said, pushing a plate with three full crepes in front of the vacant seat next to Everly's, then she looked meaningfully at her, using her head and small hand movements to encourage more conversation.

"I'm going to head out too," Olivia said, moving around the counter. "We have a video conference with the business zoning commissioner. He's heading out of town for the holiday and won't be back until the second week in January, so we can't miss it." She walked over and pulled a wine-colored quilted parka with a fur hood similar to Penelope's from the peg near the kitchen door and strung her arms through it. "Hopefully, my husband is back in his office making sure our internet connection is strong and secure despite this horribly beautiful weather."

"He was headed in when I came over here," Grayson assured her.

"Wonderful."

Everly stood to say goodbye to these women she'd known for less than an hour, but who felt like lifelong friends.

"And then," Olivia said, holding out her arms for a hug, "I might just sit down and write. You have inspired me, Miss Everly Quinn. I think maybe it's time for Aidan to get his happily ever after."

Penelope also came over to hug her. "It may not be under the best of circumstances," she whispered, "but we're glad you're here." She squeezed.

They left, and the barn fell oddly quiet.

Grayson and Everly finished their breakfast in silence.

After a few minutes, the sheriff stood.

"Are you finished?" he asked, reaching for her plate.

"Yes, thank you."

He took them over to the sink, but instead of leaving them there, he pulled the soap-filled sponge dispenser down from the rack and began to wash.

Everly jumped up, grabbed the bread towel from the

stove, and stood next to him, waiting. When he finished washing one plate, he handed it to her and she dried it, then set it down on the counter, unsure where it belonged.

"Thank you, by the way," she offered. "I'm sorry I didn't say it enough earlier. I don't know what I would have done if you hadn't found me when you did."

"You did thank me. And besides the fact that it is literally my job to make sure no one freezes to death on my watch, I'm glad we met. You intrigue me."

"You're intrigued by women who travel in blizzard conditions with no coat, no food, no phone—that's charged anyway, and no plan?"

He laughed out loud.

"What can I say? I have a type." He handed her the last dish, then reached out to dry his hands on her towel, his fingers brushing up against hers. He took it from her and set it down on the counter along with the newly dried plate.

"Scatterbrained? Impulsive? Unprepared?" she mumbled. She was almost afraid to meet his eyes. If someone had asked her yesterday, those would not have been the qualities she would have used to describe herself, but something in the last twenty-four hours had changed. She couldn't describe it.

"Rare." Grayson's voice commanded her attention, and she raised her gaze to meet his.

"Authentic." He took a step closer, daring her to back away.

"Distinctive." He reached up to brush a strand of hair away from her face and tucked it behind her ear.

"Beautiful." His fingertips lightly grazed the side of her neck, his thumb gently caressing her chin as he pulled her even closer.

Her hands instinctively moved to his waist.

"Grayson." His name spilled from her lips almost as a plea. For what, she was unsure.

A musical chime sounded just before Cass's voice came

on through one of the devices on the counter.

"Grayson, are you over there?"

His eyes fluttered, his jaw clenched, then the dimples appeared in his cheeks as he smiled, and he slid his hand down her arm and rested it at her hip, but he didn't let go of her. Didn't back away.

"Yes, Mother, I'm here."

"Oh, good. Has Everly settled in?"

"Hi, Cass," she called out. "I'm feeling right at home. Thank you." She didn't take her eyes off Grayson's, grateful she'd brushed her teeth and hoped there was no food stuck in them now.

"That's wonderful to hear. Hey, I know you kids are getting ready to wrap those gifts, but before you do that, will you just make a list of all the presents in that box? Then, if you could just write what they are on a sticky note and put it on the gift after it is wrapped that would be most appreciated. Something has come up and—need to switch a few things around, so I—be bringing—you over a few more things. I hope—" the device skipped, "—all right."

"You're coming over?" Grayson asked, dropping his head and shaking it back and forth. "When?" His voice sounded a little deflated.

"I imagine—" her voice cut out again, "—hour—the others—"

"Mom?"

The connection had dropped.

Everly stood up on her toes, hoping he could see the smile in her eyes. With a kiss on his cheek, she slid her hands down into his.

"Come on," she said, tugging lightly, pleased when his dimples returned.

Grayson held her gaze for a few more moments, an air of mischief brimming there. "This," he said, squeezing her hands, "isn't finished."

"Promise?"

He groaned.

They headed into the living room where several rolls of different varieties of wrapping paper had been set up against the couch next to the box of toys. Tape, ribbon, and several pairs of scissors had been scattered across the low wooden table that sat at the center of the furniture. Everly opened one of the drawers and was happy to find a white legal pad and a gaggle of pens.

She's a writer all right.

Grayson pushed the table away from them and closer to the fireplace, then reached over and slid the large box of gifts closer where it would be easier to see the contents.

Everly curled her legs up beneath her and clicked the pen. "What do we got?"

Both front doors slid open, and gusts of wind and snow blew into the room. The tip of a pine tree made its entrance, followed by a mixture of voices, both male and female, chatting and laughing.

Grayson shot up from the couch and ran over to help his family as they attempted to bring another gigantic tree into the barn. Everly stood. At any moment, she half expected someone to pinch her, and she'd wake up with her head on her desk at work drooling over whatever reports she'd been working on or face first in whatever microwaved dish she'd thrown in for lunch. But she wasn't at work. She was in Silver Falls, Colorado, with complete strangers who had already gained a place in her heart. This…this was real and something very different than to what she was accustomed. And she was beginning to like different.

She hustled over to the door.

"How can I help?"

Grayson stared up at the empty tree. It wasn't as large as the fir Olivia had picked out for the barn, but it was still a decent size—at least eight feet if he was guessing.

"That tree isn't going to decorate itself, Gray," Holden called, his face scrunched as he sketched out patterns for paper snowflakes in front of the fireplace.

"Why are we decorating another tree?"

Landon shrugged. "Mom said she would explain everything when she gets here."

"I don't think we're supposed to decorate it," Penelope said. "Just make the decorations to go on it."

They'd already taken care of Guardian business this year, but if he'd had to guess, it would be that his mother had found another family in need.

At first, Grayson had wondered how Liv and Pen had convinced his brothers to spend the day working on Christmas activities for their mother, and then he realized it had probably been the other way around. Holden had been dying for a reason to get the sleigh out to take it for a drive, and Landon was a sucker for hot cocoa and Granddad's Christmas cookies.

They pulled two six-foot tables from storage and set them up in the living room near the coziness of the fire. One glance over at Everly, who sat on the opposite side of the table, had his stomach all tied up in knots. Freshly popped corn, cranberries, pinecones, ribbons, and a small bag of flocking all sat on the table in front of her, ready to be made into tree decorations.

He walked around the table and pulled out the chair next to her.

"Watch and learn," he said, fingers clasped, his arms stretched. He picked up a needle and proceeded to thread it.

First try.

"You've done this before," Everly said with a hint of admiration.

"Yes, ma'am. Though, generally it takes a couple of tries

with these." He held up his hands and flexed his fingers. "The trick is in the string. It's so much easier with a fresh cut on the end."

Before too long he had several kernels of popped corn lined up on his garland.

"Ouch." Everly shook one hand and shoved an offending thumb into her mouth.

"Here, let me see." Grayson held out his palm.

She glanced at him momentarily before finally showing him.

He examined her thumb. It was a little red and several needle impressions still lingered there.

"There's not even any blood, ya big baby," he said with a laugh.

She tried to snatch it back, feigning offense, but he held firm. "You should have started with the popcorn," he said, glancing over at his own strand. "Cranberries tend to be a little tougher to get through. But if you insist on working with them…" he reached over and picked up one of the metal thimbles from the sewing box and slipped it onto the tip of her thumb, "then I highly recommend using one of these."

"Good tip." Everly looked down at her latest casualty—a three-quarter berry. "Do you think it's salvageable?"

Without thinking about it, Grayson picked it up from the table and popped it into his mouth. The last time he'd had cranberries was last Thanksgiving in Aunt Kathlene's marshmallow cranberry salad. He'd forgotten just how bitter and sharp they could be by themselves. As he chewed, his face contorted, and one eye closed to compensate for the tart flavor.

"They are," he swallowed, "delicious."

"Convincing," Everly laughed as she took one directly from the bowl and popped it into her own mouth.

"No!" Everyone at the table screamed out in unison.

Nothing. Not one wince or grimace.

She smiled.

"They're even better right off the bush." A grin spread across her face.

Impressive.

"One point for Everly," Holden called out with a chuckle. And she ate another for good measure.

"Oh, we're keeping score now?" she asked with a raised brow.

"Show off," Grayson said, reaching into the bowl of popcorn and tossing a handful at her.

They bounced and landed in disarray on the table in front of her, but she didn't move, and her facial expression remained stoic, suddenly unsmiling. Grayson's eyes widened as he looked over at his sister-in-law, scrunched his shoulders, and raised his hands.

Had he misread her?

Everly picked up one of the kernels.

"Did you know that popped corn pieces are actually called flakes? One like this," she held up the kernel, "is called a mushroom flake because it has this rounded top and very few wispy edges," she said right before she tossed it at him, hitting him directly between the eyes.

Penelope laughed. "Point two."

Everly picked up another one. "This one would be considered a butterfly flake because of its irregular shape and little wispy bits kind of like wings," she said, folding her lips to poorly hide her smile, and flicked it at his ear.

She missed.

The third time, he was prepared. "Mushroom flakes tend to be more flavorful because they hold the butter, or caramel, or other types of flavorings well, while the butterfly flakes are said to have a better mouth feel." The moment she tossed the kernel at him, he tilted back just enough that he was able to catch it in his mouth.

He raised his hands in the air, satisfied when a soft giggle escaped her lips.

"Definitely a butterfly," he said as the white puffiness seemed to melt in his mouth.

She threw one more piece at him for good measure.

"How do you know that?" Olivia asked. "I may or may not need to use it in one of my books."

"Years ago, a good friend of mine taught me how to make caramel, and I used that knowledge to make several varieties—including caramel corn—to help me get through school. Mushroom flakes make the best caramel corn."

"You must have been a very popular person around Christmastime."

"It's been a long time since I have done anything like this for the holidays. I forgot just how much fun it can be."

"Especially when you are doing it with the right people." Grayson looked over at her, noting the kernel that had gotten stuck in her curls. He couldn't help but reach over to pull it from her hair.

When she met his eyes, he saw a glimpse of loneliness there, buoyed up by strength, wonder, and hope. But there was something else that he couldn't quite put his finger on.

"All right, you two, those strands are not going to string themselves." Penelope pushed the bowl of cranberries closer to them.

Everly put the thimble back on her thumb and held it up for him to see.

He handed her a gripper pad.

"This will make it easier for you to actually pull the needle through." He picked up his own needle and thimble, took a cranberry from the bowl, pushed the needle partway through, then used the gripper pad on the top portion of the needle below the point to pull it the rest of the way through. "It goes much faster when you aren't pricking your fingers or causing blisters."

"Another great tip."

With all of them working on the décor, they made quick work of it, and by lunchtime, they had all the garlands strung, hundreds of snowflakes cut out, wooden disks sanded and drilled, and ornaments with pinecones, small boughs, and ribbon glued and flocked.

A thud on the barn doors had all three brothers up in moments. Landon took one door and Grayson took the other. When they slid them open, their mom would have fallen onto the floor had Holden not been there to catch her, but some of the bags she carried had not been so lucky. Oranges rolled in several directions at once. Cans of yams and cranberries tumbled from the paper grocery sack along with dozens of potatoes.

The women all scrambled to help.

"What's with all the food? Are we prepping a pre-Christmas dinner?" Holden asked, righting their mother to her feet.

"Thank you, dear," Cass said as she shook off the snow from her coat and stepped into the barn. "It's not for us."

"Is it safe?" their father asked from the doorway, standing behind a stack of boxes he held from the length of his arms to his chin.

"Here, let me help you with those." Grayson took all but the very bottom box from his father. "Why didn't you let us know you were here? We would have come outside and helped you in with all of this."

"Oh, there's more." Benjamin Kane walked over to the empty space on one of the tables and set down his load. "It's a good thing that snowcoach has a backseat."

Grayson peeked outside. The weather had settled for the moment, but drifts had piled up high against the barn, and the light pink hues in the sky promised more snowfall. He smiled, grateful for a little more time to get to know the beauty who had just crashed into his life, and he looked over his shoulder to where his sisters-in-law were huddled around her in conversation.

Landon pulled his side of the barn closed, but as Grayson reached for the handle on the opposite door, he noted another snowmobile as it came around the fence, two large sacks strung like saddlebags over his tail end.

"Granddad is nothing if not inventive," he said aloud.

So much for spending a quiet afternoon alone with Everly.

It was a good thing that he loved his family and was also grateful for the time he had to spend with them. He waited for the older man to pull up to the winter garage, but he drove the sled right up to the barn doors.

"Not going to tromp through all this snow if I can help it," Ian said, hoisting up the bags and carrying them over his shoulder like Santa.

He'd let his white beard grow quite long over the last year, so he definitely fit the part. Grayson had actually heard one of Olivia's fans from her last reader retreat refer to him as 'some sort of sexy Santa in blue jeans and a cattleman's jacket.' He laughed out loud at the thought.

Go, Granddad.

With foodstuffs all laid out on the large island in the kitchen, boxes of presents needing to be wrapped spread out on the tables, and the finished Christmas decorations all packaged up into several apple crates, Grayson sat down on the floor in front of Everly on the couch and looked up at his mother.

"It was brought to my attention last night that Matt Gusterson has been out of work for a few months now, and they have to be out of their place shortly after Christmas," Cass said, her brows furrowed and her hands wringing. "With their two littles and one on the way, I thought we could extend our Guardian adventures this year and help out another family in need."

Called it.

"What does he do?" Ian leaned forward in his chair.

"When is she due?" Olivia asked.

"How old are the children?" Penelope tilted her head, the wheels already turning.

Grayson loved his family, but was never more proud of them than at Christmastime. He saw a lot of bad things in his job, and unfortunately, they seemed to get harder around the holidays. The Guardian tradition had been around for generations, apparently having started nearly six generations ago.

Ting. Ting. Ting.

His jingle-bell ringtone for work sounded.

He pulled his phone from his pocket.

Silver Springs Police Department.

"If you'll excuse me a moment, I need to take this." Grayson pushed himself up off the floor and headed into the kitchen.

"Yeah, Janie, what's up?"

"Look, Sheriff, I know it's your day off, but Frank Collins is in the hospital. I thought you'd want to know."

"What happened?"

"Someone broke into his shop. He took a tire iron to the back of the head. His daughter found him and called the paramedics."

His free hand balled into a fist. That is not what he'd expected. A failing lift maybe or jammed tools. Not violence. Not in Silver Falls. Not again.

"You were right to call. Thank you."

"Gray, he's in pretty bad shape. With this storm, it took them over an hour to get to him."

Grayson's jaw clenched.

"Understood. Where is Marcus?"

"Deputy Gonzalez is out on another call. I'll keep trying him."

"Thanks, Janie. I'll get Wesley and head over there right now. Let Marcus know and have him join us when he can."

"Yes, sir."

After Olivia's stalker, and the incident with the man who'd hunted down Penelope and shot Landon, Grayson had deputized his granddad and his cousin to help out whenever needed. It had come in handy several times—especially for things like the Christmas festival, but it had been a while since they were needed for something like this.

He called Wes who was more than eager to get out of pie-baking with his mother. So many of the town's people were still counting on the festival, but with just two days to go, he wasn't so sure that would be happening. His cousin just lived up at SilverHawk, which would make it easy to collect him on his way into town.

Grayson shoved his phone back into his pocket.

"I have to go," he said, walking back into the living room, picking up his coat that had been draped over one of the overstuffed chairs.

"You're leaving?" Everly said, standing up from her place on the couch.

"Someone broke into Frank's shop, and he's hurt pretty bad." He turned to face Everly. "Frank is the mechanic who was working on your Courier."

"Oh, no. I hope he's all right." She placed a hand on his arm.

Grayson covered her hand with his own.

"It's not looking good."

He started forward as if he would kiss her goodbye, then caught himself. It felt so...so normal to have her around, he had to remind himself that she was still a virtual stranger, and he had much to learn about her—though, admittedly, he looked forward to that.

"I'll be back as soon as I can. Hopefully, in time to do the Guardian run," he said with a glance over at his mother. Then, he looked over at Landon. "And don't eat all of Granddad's cookies while I'm gone."

Landon raised his hands in the air. "No promises."

With a nod at his family, Grayson headed to the door. His granddad followed.

"You stay here on this one, Granddad. Wes is waiting on me." He shoved his feet into his boots and retrieved his Stetson from the rack. "I need you to keep an eye out and make sure everyone here stays safe."

"You call me if you need anything, son." Ian handed his grandson the keys to the snowmobile. "I have a feeling we'll be here for a bit, and it looks like it's itching to do some more snowing before long."

A concerned smile from Everly put a little flutter in Grayson's chest when he dared one more look, and he smiled back. He jumped on his granddad's snowmobile and drove it the short distance to the winter garage on the other side of the barn where they stored his snowcat. Normally, his truck or even a snowmobile would have sufficed, but with the uncertainty of this weather, he didn't want to chance getting caught out in it.

Who would do something like this? During a blizzard?

His gut said there was trouble afoot, and his gut was rarely wrong.

CHAPTER EIGHT

A pit dropped in Everly's stomach with a glimpse at reality. Grayson Kane was a sheriff—not just the save you from a snowbank type of sheriff or the help organize events type of sheriff or even a feel-good Christmas movie sheriff, but he was a man who put his life on the line every day to keep others protected type of sheriff. While she admired and appreciated their contributions, she'd found out firsthand the sacrifices that had to be made to the job by both officers and loved ones, and she never wanted to experience that kind of loss again. The job had taken her father away from their family long before the high-speed crash that had claimed his life.

What are you doing?

She glanced around at his wonderful family, noting the look in his mother's eye when he left. It was the same look her own mother had worn many a late night after her father had been called in to handle a situation. Everly could not fall for a man in law enforcement. It brought too much worry, doubt, fear, and inevitably, pain.

Too late. She pushed the thought deep down, grabbed the pillow sitting next to her on the couch, and shoved it over her face.

She needed to talk to Violet.

When Cass finished laying out their plans to deliver a full-blown Christmas complete with a tree and all its decorations, a four-course feast, and a Santa sack full of gifts to this down-on-their-luck family, Everly realized her meager contributions at the foster center paled by comparison.

"And don't you worry, Everly," she said, "the girls have got some winter clothes that I think will suit you just fine."

This family was something right out of a fairytale book. They planned Christmas festivals, had their own recipes for hot apple cider, and they even delivered gifts to needy families for the holidays—despite a blizzard. And they were including her as if she'd been a part of the family for years.

Seriously, who are these people?

"Sounds great. Um, will you just excuse me for a moment, please?" she said, pushing herself up off the couch.

Once she was out of view, she stopped and threw herself up against the wall, trying to catch her breath. Everything seemed to be coming at her a million miles a minute. Just twenty-four hours ago she was employed, had a functioning vehicle, and had plans for Christmas—fuzzy socks with hot peppermint cocoa, cashew chicken and wontons from Panda Garden, and watching the holiday romance movie marathon had all sounded like heaven. Most of all, her heart had been safe. But now, all that had changed.

"Do you think we scared her off?"

Everly could still hear them talking in the living room.

"Maybe we should go check on her."

"Give her a minute." Olivia's voice was unmistakable. "The Kanes can be a lot to handle at Christmas. I'm sure she is just processing. She only has one sister and I get the impression that they don't always spend the holidays together, so this must be overwhelming."

Everly couldn't listen anymore.

How could the people she'd just met understand her
better than half the relationships she'd had over the past few
years?

Across the hall was a door that led out onto a veranda
similar to the one outside her room. She slipped it open and
stepped outside. While the air was chilled, she welcomed the
fresh air into her lungs. It must have been the position of the
veranda, but it seemed that the drifts that had blown through
had taken snow off the deck and railing instead of depositing it
there. She stepped closer to the edge and leaned down onto
the railing with her forearms, glancing out over the vast
property with all of its evergreens, aspens, and outbuildings.

A sort of clicking sound mixed with several grunts and
snorts caught her attention. She glanced just to her left, and
there, not eight feet away stood a reindeer.

She gasped in awe but didn't dare move for fear she might
scare it away. It had antlers, and Everly had remembered
reading somewhere that only the female reindeer retained their
antlers in winter. She'd never seen one of them up close, and
was admittedly surprised that this animal's coloring was more
gray than brown. It contrasted beautifully with the landscape
behind it.

Penelope will be sad she missed this.

"You must belong to Santa," she said quietly, trying not to
feel silly for talking to her.

The snow nearly reached the reindeer's underbelly, but she
didn't seem to mind, and she turned and looked directly at her,
then she laid down in the snow as if it was the most natural
thing in the world for her to do.

Everly held her breath.

All the world seemed so still at this moment. A soft breeze
combed through her hair, and she briskly rubbed her arms
against the cold. She'd do well not to stay out here too long, or
she would catch her death—just what she needed right now.

A few more grunts alerted Everly to a group of them that

maneuvered just beyond the tree line.

"Beautiful creatures, aren't they?"

"Mr. Redbourne, you startled me."

"Eh, none of this Mr. Redbourne stuff. You can call me Ian. Or Granddad if you prefer. Everybody does." He tossed a fluffy blanket around her shoulders and handed her a mug of steaming hot cocoa before leaning up against the railing.

"Thank you."

"I hope you don't mind the intrusion."

"Of course not."

"I enjoy it when the reindeer come around this time of year."

"I didn't know there were reindeer in Colorado." She had always imagined they lived closer to the North Pole, Alaska maybe or even Greenland, but not Colorado. The thought seemed silly now.

"There's a reindeer farm not too far from here. We let them roam on our land."

"I can see why they want to stay," she said with appreciation. "It's beautiful here."

"That it is. That it is."

Several moments of silence passed between them.

"I just needed a little air. I hope that's all right." Everly hoped she hadn't been rude when she'd left.

Ian turned around, leaning his back against the railing, and looked at her, his arms folded.

"It's a little different than what you're used to?"

"You could say that."

"Small family?"

Everly nodded. "It's just me and my sister now."

"I'm sorry."

"Don't be," Everly said with a soft smile. "We've made it work."

Granddad dipped his head in understanding but didn't say anything more.

Lifting the ceramic mug to her lips, Everly took a sip of her cocoa, grateful for the trail of warmth that descended to her belly.

"Do you ever…worry…"

"About my grandson?"

He knew. How did he know?

"We have one in every generation."

"One?"

"A lawman." Ian stood up and turned to look at her. "Sometimes two."

She wasn't sure if it was from the weather or because it was like he could see right into her soul, but she pulled the blanket a little tighter around her shoulders to curb the chills that cascaded from head to toe.

"I don't know if I can do this." Her chest tightened and tears threatened.

How had this man, this sheriff, had such an effect on her? How could she possibly love him after just one day?

"You've had your share of loss. I can see that." One eye squinted a little as if Ian could assess her life just by looking at her.

"My father."

"Was a lawman?"

"Yep." She sniffled, *mostly* from the cold.

"You know, darlin'," Ian said placing a hand over hers, "life has a way of bringin' folks together just when they least expect it, but when they need it most." He lowered his head to meet her eyes. "Grayson is a good man with a good heart, I suspect that is why he chose to work where he felt he could do the most good. Don't let past fears rob you of a chance at something great."

Everly wiped a single tear that had spilled down onto her cheek.

He let her go and stepped toward the door before turning back. "Now, I didn't know your daddy none, but I do know my grandson, and if you feel about him the way I suspect he's feeling about you…it's worth the risk. Love is always worth the risk." He paused, his eyes lingering on hers for a solid poignant moment, then closed the door behind him.

With a tightened grip on the blanket around her shoulders, she took another sip of her cocoa.

Love?

Parts of her face were starting to go numb, but she still needed to check in with her sister. Her fingers trembled as she dialed.

"Everly! Merry almost Christmas, sis," Violet said when she answered the phone.

It was so good to hear her voice.

"Merry almost Christmas." She tried to keep the emotion from her voice, but she'd never been very good at masking her feelings and tended to wear them on her sleeve.

"Is everything all right?" Her sister had always been too intuitive for her own good.

"Yes, of course," she lied. "I um, kind of, met someone." She brushed the snow off the small table and set down her mug, then brushed off a little section of the chair next to it.

"You what? Where? How? Who? You must tell me everything."

"He's…I don't know, just everything I've ever wanted in a man." She felt the seat of the chair, but it was just too wet and cold to sit. "And…the one thing I didn't."

"Too short?"

"No," Everly scoffed as she thought of Grayson's six-foot-plus stature.

"Poor?"

"What? No. Violet," she protested, shaking her head, but grateful for the humor her sister had injected into the conversation. "He's…a sheriff." She said the last word almost in a whisper.

"Okaaay, and what? Has he eaten one too many donuts?"

Violet laughed at her own little joke.

"And nothing. He's a sheriff, Vi, and I just don't know if I can let myself fall for him."

"You mean because of Dad?"

"Yes, because of Dad. He left us, Vi."

"No, Ev. He died."

Another tear trailed her face, which she quickly swiped away with the back of her hand.

Stop it.

"What if…?"

"Your sheriff dies too?"

Everly nodded—even though she knew her sister couldn't see her.

"How do you feel about him?"

"It's hard to explain. We only just met, but when I'm with him, he feels like…home. Is that weird?" She brought her thumb to her mouth and chewed lightly on her thumbnail.

"Does he feel the same way?"

"I don't know." Everly threw her arm in the air, knocking the blanket from her shoulder. "Maybe. But his family seems to think so."

"Wait, you've met his family?" Violet's surprise was endearing. "Didn't you say you just met?"

"I'm actually kind of…staying with them at the moment," she said, pulling the blanket back up around her. "It's a long story."

"Wait, my sister is spending the holidays somewhere other than at work or in her apartment eating takeout and watching romance movies?" Violet knew her all too well. "Marry this man."

"Violet!"

"What? Life isn't worth anything, Ev, if you're not willing to take a chance. I know you got your heart broken before and it has taken you a long time to get over what happened—wait, you are over him, right?"

"Of course, I am."

"Whew. Okay, then, where was I? Oh, yes, I know you got your heart broken before and it has taken you a long time to get over what he did to you, but sometimes the risks are what make the reward so sweet. If this sheriff—"

"Grayson. His name is Grayson." It sounded as if Violet had rehearsed this speech a thousand times.

"If *Grayson* feels like home to you—if he makes you want to live the romance instead of wallowing in your singleness and watching it on TV, then Everly Quinn, what is stopping you from taking that chance? From living your life?"

A snowflake landed on one of Everly's eyelashes. She blinked several times and then looked heavenward. It wasn't like they didn't get snow in Albuquerque, but being nestled up in this little mountain town, where the worries of city life had seemed to melt away, it felt different.

He felt different.

Maybe it was time to take a chance again. What happened with Eli was a long time ago, and sheriff or not, Grayson was the kind of different she wanted in her life.

Tap. Tap.

Everly turned around to see Olivia tapping on the glass pane of the door.

"Listen, Vi, I've got to go, but I'll call you later, all right?"

"You better. Hey, Ev…"

"What?"

"You got this."

"Thanks, sis. Love you."

"Love you."

With a quick exhale, Everly picked up her now cold mug and slipped back into the house. As the warmth greeted her a chill cascaded down her body as it acclimated.

"Everything all right?" Olivia asked.

"Yes, sorry. That was my sister. I just realized that I probably won't get to see her for Christmas is all. But, um, I'm fine."

"You know what we say in this house about 'fine'?"

"What's that?"

"That *fine* is...well, never fine." She put an arm around Everly's shoulders. "Come on, we have something for you."

When she walked back out into the living room, only Penelope remained.

"Where did everyone go?"

"They're loading up the sleigh," Penelope said dismissively as if that was something normally said in everyday conversation.

"I'm not even going to ask."

A sleigh?

At this point, nothing would surprise her about this family.

"You can't very well go about Guardian business in yoga pants and a raglan tee—not that whoever picked them out doesn't have great taste," Olivia smiled. "—but you'll freeze."

Laid out on the couch were several articles of clothing—jeans, sweaters, jackets, socks, beanie caps, and even a couple of pairs of different-sized boots.

"I hope you don't mind. We picked out a couple of outfits that we thought might fit and would keep you warm tonight."

Everly was touched.

"But how did you get them here?"

"We live like a hundred feet up the road. A little snow wasn't going to stop us."

"I don't know what to say. You have all been so kind and generous already."

"You should try them on," Penelope encouraged, picking up the cream-colored cashmere sweater and holding it out to her.

"Now?" she asked, reaching for the top.

"Yes. Now. Go!"

The excited look on their faces, and their hearty

encouragement, made Everly feel a little giddy. She and Violet had treated themselves to shopping and lunch on occasion, and they'd always had a wonderful time being together, but this was different somehow. Vi had her own group of friends that had been very close all through high school. Everly had been friendly enough and was friends with people from many different groups, but had never really felt like she'd found 'her tribe.'

She imagined that this was exactly what it felt like to have friends who were genuinely interested in her and with whom she could try on clothes, drink cocoa, and spend an afternoon chatting and wrapping gifts. She liked it.

"What exactly are we doing tonight?" she called from her room.

She'd heard Grayson use the term Guardian Run, but she wasn't sure what that meant.

"And what is a Guardian?" she asked, peeking around the door.

The two women exchanged glances and smiled.

"You'll see."

CHAPTER NINE

"Hey, Shauna," Grayson leaned onto the counter-tall information desk at the hospital, "could you give me Frank Collins' room number please?" He'd known the nurse since they'd worked together on the Forensics Science Club council in High School.

"I'm sorry, Sheriff, but Mr. Collins is being prepped for surgery. They had to call in a surgeon from Denver who's been held up on account of the snow." She pointed at a young woman in the waiting room. "But his daughter over there is the one who brought him in."

"Thank you," he said, tapping the desk. "I owe you one."

"Or three," she called after him.

After twenty minutes of speaking with Frank's daughter, he and Wesley headed back to the shop. Unfortunately, she hadn't been able to provide them with much information as her father had been unconscious when she found him. However, she had noticed an unfamiliar car parked just down the street from her father's shop. She said she wouldn't have paid much attention to it except that, unlike any of the other vehicles around the area, it had not been covered in snow and all the shops near there had been closed.

"A black sedan is not much to go on," Wes said, "though,

I do wonder how a sedan was able to travel on these roads."

When they pulled up in front of the shop, it was easy to see where the emergency vehicles had pulled up to the building as the roads had been plowed in a single path.

Grayson pointed to a black sedan parked on a side street around the corner. However, now the vehicle had accumulated several inches of snow.

"What are the odds?" Wes jumped down off the snowcat with his camera. "I'll check it out."

"Be careful." Grayson made his way around the perimeter of the shop. As he approached the side door, he noted a trail of deep, uneven tracks in the freshly fallen snow. The wooden shutters on the top half of the door sat open, the window missing.

Point of entry.

Streaks of red smeared across the icy landscape, but were fading quickly under the continuous onslaught of powder falling from the skies.

Blood.

Grayson pulled a small plastic jar from his jacket and scooped up a sample of the evidence before it became too diluted. He tucked it into his interior pocket, then carefully cleared the snow from the base of the door. Without having done so initially, the intruder would have had to both come in and leave through the broken window.

Upon closer examination, small shards of jagged glass still embedded in the side of the window frame had been stained with blood.

What could possibly be worth so much effort to break into a small-town mechanic shop? Frank wasn't a wealthy man—he wouldn't have a lot of cash on hand, and the vehicles currently in his shop wouldn't fetch much of a price, so why would someone be so stupid as to break in through a window in broad daylight? He looked up into the ever-darkening, snow-filled sky.

"Maybe more like narrow daylight? Limited daylight?"

Who was he kidding, visibility would have been just as poor or worse than if it were full-on midnight. He used the tweezers from his toolkit to pull out the stained shard of glass and slipped it into another container.

"Talking to ourselves now, are we?" Wes laughed as he made his way to the door. He snapped a few pictures.

"Just thinking aloud." Grayson chuckled.

"That's enough blood that someone is going to require stitches. We should probably check in with the clinic downtown."

"We'll have Marcus do that as soon as he gets here. You find anything?"

"Car is registered to a R&J Holdings out of New Mexico."

Grayson looked up at his cousin and narrowed his eyes.

What are the chances?

"Albuquerque?" he asked.

"Yeah, how did you know?"

His heart sank. He dropped his head with a shake.

"Just a hunch."

Of course, it couldn't just be easy.

Everly had intrigued him from the moment she'd climbed out of her little matchbox. The timing had been too convenient, their connection too perfect. He needed to get inside. Though it seemed improbable that his beautiful new friend had had anything to do with this break-in, he had learned a long time ago that coincidences were rarely that. He slipped on his leather gloves and opened the door.

Electricity hummed overhead as Grayson turned on the lights inside the shop, casting eerie shadows on the grease-stained floor. Everly's little red truck sat in bay two at ground level, the passenger door ajar. Tools lay scattered across the concrete and trinkets of all sorts cluttered the ground—an office stapler, several pens and pads of paper, a stainless-steel water bottle, and a set of keys among them. He stepped over the mess, careful not to disturb anything before Wes could get pictures.

It appeared as if the contents of a banker's box had been emptied on the floor of the truck. The intruder had been looking for something, but what? He picked up a plaque and turned it over.

In recognition of
Everly Quinn
for showing
Outstanding Leadership
in the Community

Impressive.

He set it down and picked up another. This time, a chunk of acrylic.

"In honor of a remarkable individual," he read aloud, "whose unwavering commitment to bettering the world has empowered countless others to create positive changes in their lives and their communities, fostered hope in those who had once lost it, and inspired others to believe in the possibilities of tomorrow. Everly Quinn, Outstanding Achievement."

What is all this?

She'd opted to bring awards and office supplies with her to Colorado, but hadn't given a second thought to bringing a coat or even a change of clothes? The gears in his mind churned with potential scenarios—none of which made a whole lot of sense, but ideas were formulating. The irony was not lost on him. He'd never had a connection with a woman the way he'd felt connected to Everly. She'd literally fallen into his arms—thanks to her strappy sandals in the snow. And yet here he was, knee deep in an investigation with her name literally written all over it.

He chuckled, despite himself.

He recalled the defeated expression on her face when she'd landed on her rear-end in the snow when they'd left the inn, the awe in her eyes when she'd seen the inside of the barn, and the sassy side of her come out when she'd tossed his popcorn back in his face. And then, that moment, when they stood alone in the kitchen, a loose tendril falling in front of her beautiful eyes…he'd seen her so unsure of herself, self-deprecating, humble, yet as he'd traced the contours of her cheek and heard that tiny inhalation of air, he'd seen in her his future. He'd never wanted to kiss a woman more than he had in that moment.

"It looks like the perp was focused on this little beater." Wes yanked him back from his thoughts, indicating the truck with his chin—the click of his camera distinct in the otherwise silent garage.

Grayson cleared his throat, refocusing his mind on the task at hand. "I think you've been watching too much TV, Wesley. We don't really call them 'perps.'" Grayson chuckled as he moved aside to allow his cousin to photograph the scene, though the award remained in his hand.

"Like I have time for excess television," Wes retorted with feigned hurt. "I think the *suspect*," he emphasized the proper term, "broke in solely for this vehicle." He opened the glove box and pulled out the registration. "It looks like it belongs to an—"

"Everly Quinn. I know."

"How," Wes peeked his head from the truck, "do you do that?"

Grayson's mind whirled.

Why would someone randomly break into the oldest vehicle in Frank's shop and go through a box full of random office supplies and pictures?

The most obvious answer was simple. It wasn't random.

It appeared as if she had cleared out the contents of a work desk. Maybe she had just quit or was fired from some job. But then why would she bring it with her on a road trip? Thinking of her coatless and ill-prepared for the weather, things were starting to make a little more sense.

She'd been let go.

Though why losing a job had triggered her to travel hundreds of miles through a blizzard was still a mystery.

"Found her last night after she'd been run off the road by a pickup at Kneaders Fork," he finally replied. "She'd been diverted off the highway on her way to Estes Park."

"Thus, the truck, if you can even call this little thing a truck, is in the shop." Wes tapped on the roof.

Grayson nodded as he picked up a framed picture of two women embracing with huge smiles spread across their faces, immediately recognizing Everly's likeness in the beautifully candid shot. The other woman in the picture was also very pretty. Her hair was lighter, but they had very similar features. He guessed her to be the sister with whom she was supposed to be spending the holidays.

"So, where is this woman now?" Wes asked. "I spoke to Rachel earlier today and she told me that for the first time since last Christmas, the inn is completely full."

"That it is." The words came out of his mouth, but his thoughts were focused elsewhere.

Was there something that Everly wasn't telling him? He'd generally prided himself on being a good judge of character, but had his heart blinded him to something more…nefarious? After looking around for a few more minutes, Grayson agreed with Wes's initial assessment that Everly's truck had been the only thing targeted.

"It'll be difficult to get Miss Quinn to come down to the station until the roads are plowed, but I do happen to know where she is staying." Her box with all its contents had just become evidence and therefore could not be out of his custody until it was logged properly. "Would you like to accompany me for a little Guardian business? We can talk to her there."

"Guardian business?" Wesley's brows scrunched together.

"You mean she is with your family?" He took one last shot of the interior of the truck before shutting the door. "I thought you said you just met her."

"I did."

"And you already trust her with Guardian business?"

"I did trust her. Do…trust her," he corrected, wanting to give her the benefit of the doubt. "There is just something about her, you know? Special."

Grayson picked up the box with her things and set it down on the counter next to the door.

"It sounds weird, even to me, but I felt something. A connection with her." Why he was explaining his feelings to Wes was beyond him.

Though, he chalked it up to possibility, *it could just be pheromones.*

Even as he thought it, he knew it wasn't true. There was more to this story, and he intended to find out what—as the sheriff and as a man.

"You like this woman. Like a lot like this woman. Does Olivia know?" Wes asked as he packed his camera back into the bag. "You realize this just may be fodder for her next book, right?"

With several evidence bags and vials, along with the contents of Everly's truck, they headed back out to the cat.

Gertrude had just pulled up in her huge truck, lights flashing out by the abandoned sedan.

Wes shrugged. "It was illegally parked."

Not that the driver would have been able to get far in what looked like a now bottomed-out car, but now he, or she, he reckoned, would be on foot. And there were limited places for him to go—here to the mechanic shop, or over to the diner, the bank, and Cal's veterinary clinic across the street.

Just as Gertrude finished lowering the flatbed on the back of her truck, Grayson waited for that movie moment when a man would come running out of the diner, trudging through the deep snow and across the street toward her, dressed in a long waistcoat and a cabbie cap, arguing for her to stop.

He waited.

Nothing.

That would have been too easy.

He chuckled as he set Everly's box inside the snowcat, but before he pulled himself up, his eyes were drawn to the café where a man he didn't recognize sat at the window sipping a hot drink. Grayson narrowed his eyes a moment, keen to observe the stranger, a mug brought to his mouth, and his eyes peering over the top as he watched as the robust tow-truck driver continued to hook her cables up to the car.

"Hey, Wes, feels like a hot cocoa kind of afternoon. Let me buy you a cup."

"Sold."

The low rumble of plow engines and the scraping of blades against the road's surface filled the air. They waited for a huge extended cab truck to pass before crossing the street. Snowflakes continued to fall, though their descent had slowed significantly over the last hour. The little bell over the diner door rang as Grayson and Wes stepped inside.

"Sheriff. Deputy," one of the waitresses greeted, "can I get you boys a cup of coffee on this fine afternoon?"

"Thanks, Darla, but we'll just take a couple of your Christmas cocoas to go please."

Grayson casually glanced over to the window, but the stranger was gone. A coffee mug sat on the table, and cash had been laid out for a tip, but there was no other indication that anyone had been there. His eyes darted around the diner, but the place was empty. How had he gotten out of there without being seen?

He walked over to the table and looked out the window. Gertrude had just finished.

"I guess the weather has made it pretty slow in here?" Grayson asked.

"You're telling me. If I could have stayed home with my feet up today in front of a fire with one of your sister-in-law's books, I would have."

"Darla, there was a man in here a few minutes ago sitting right over there. Have you ever seen him before?"

She glanced over to the table. "Coffee. Two creams, no sugar. Looked like he was from out of town with his fancy coat pulled up to his ears and brown shoes completely inappropriate for this kind of weather. Nope, never seen him before. And he didn't say much, but he did ask for the nearest hotel." She handed Grayson and Wes their drinks. "Something wrong, Sheriff?"

"No, ma'am. Just curious is all." He tipped his hat and handed her a large bill before turning on his heel. "Merry Christmas, Darla."

"Merry Christmas," she called after them.

If someone was actually looking for Everly, it wouldn't be too long before he'd find her. People in this town were nothing short of an information station on the ins and outs of everyone's lives—and a stranger in town would have their tongues wagging. He'd find out where she was staying in no time. And that was not acceptable.

They drove directly back to the homestead. Silver Springs and all his family's surrounding ranches came with their own security in the form of dozens of ranchers and ranch hands who had been prepared for emergency situations. In the last couple of years, between a stalker and a mob boss, they were no strangers to danger or trouble.

Grayson was relieved to see Granddaddy Cole's big old sleigh still parked in front of the barn. The tree had been loaded, and the tarped backseat rippled in waves of what he suspected were the decorations and wrapped gifts for the Gusterson children. Snow had been shoveled off the walks, and the roads had been plowed.

His brothers had been busy.

He pulled the cat into the snow garage.

"Before we talk to her, I'd like to get a little more background," Grayson said, as he climbed inside the Bronco.

He opened the MDC and searched for her name. Not so much as a parking ticket showed up for her. He pulled up an internet browser and searched again. This time, pages and pages of information popped up. He scanned through several articles that talked about her volunteer work in the community, some spoke of her work with several high-profile clients, but one article in particular hit him like a punch to the gut.

"Beloved Fantasy Writer Eli Thomas to Marry Media Professional Everly Quinn," he read the title out loud.

That's why she acted so weird when she found out Eli Thomas was coming.

"She's engaged?" Wes asked incredulously.

There, below the title, was a picture of the smug-looking author with Everly. Her hair was pulled to the side, and she wore thick makeup around her eyes, but it was definitely Everly. His Everly. He turned the unit around for Wesley to see.

But what could her end game possibly be? There was something more to the story. Something he was missing.

Wesley whistled. "That's her? She might just be even out of your league, Mr. December."

"I don't know what you're mocking me for. At least I didn't have to lie on the riverbank in my jeans shirtless for one of the summer months." He turned the screen back toward him. "And you're right. She is definitely out of my league."

Wesley guffawed loudly. "And it was June thank you very much."

Tap. Tap.

Grayson snapped the computer shut like he'd been looking at something he wasn't supposed to, then turned to see his mother staring up at him from outside the truck.

"Oh, good. You boys are home. What on earth are you

waiting out here for?" she asked in a muffled voice from
behind the glass, then leaned over to peer through the window
with squinted eyes. "Wesley, will you be joining us tonight?"

Grayson rolled down his window and his cousin leaned
forward.

"You know I love Guardian business, Aunt Cass.
Wouldn't miss it."

"Good, well, everything is almost loaded." She patted the
truck door and disappeared outside.

"So, what are you going to do?" Wes asked, dropping his
gaze to the closed top of Grayson's computer.

"I guess we're about to find out."

CHAPTER TEN

"This year," Olivia said as she walked out the door, "I vote that Grayson and Everly should ride in the front seat."

"Hear, hear!" Penelope agreed.

Everly had never ridden in a sleigh before and the thought of experiencing it for the first time alongside Grayson brought a smile to her lips. He had been gone for a few hours though, and she was beginning to doubt the handsome sheriff would return in time to make this delivery. The longer she was away from him, the more she thought that she had imagined it.

The snow had stopped falling for the moment, but the sky was growing darker with each passing minute. Before long, it would be nighttime and their path would be more difficult to light—especially if they decided to keep away from the main roads.

To hear everyone talking about it, being a Guardian was the best part of Christmas. And they had inducted her this year as an honorary member. No matter what happened with Grayson, she had made lifelong friends and was grateful for her experience at the ranch. The women had bundled her up nice and warm. With jeans and the cream cashmere sweater she'd chosen, which felt like heaven against her skin, they'd also provided her with a pair of brown suede, rounded-toe boots, a fur-lined coat, gloves, and a beanie cap to wear. Not only had the women prepared her more appropriately to be out in the weather, but she felt pretty. And that feeling had been gone for a long time.

Everly walked out of the barn doors and nearly right into the largest horse she had ever laid eyes on. It was the type of horse she had only ever seen in the movies. If it had wanted to, it could have rested its chin on the top of her head. Black leather tack protruded from its red-brown coat and its blonde-colored mane. She knew enough to know that they wore blinders to stop them from being spooked by things in their side vision, and right now, she was grateful.

"Her name is Duchess." Grayson's deep voice warmed her from the inside, and she whirled around to see him, his dimples on display. "Hi."

"Hi." When she met his eyes, all of the feels she'd experienced from earlier came flooding back. Sheriff or not, he'd certainly caught her attention.

"Don't be afraid." He reached up and gently stroked the horse's neck. "Here." He took her hand in his and brought it up to lay flat against the horse. "She's a sweetheart." He leaned down close to her ear. "I think she's my favorite, but don't tell Duke over there."

The feel of his hand over hers sent a new wave of chills cascading down her arms, and she shook them off.

"Cold?" he asked.

"No."

After another moment, he patted the horse's neck a couple of times and stepped back.

"I understand we've got the reins."

"I'm guessing that means we were voted into the front seat?"

Grayson laughed. "That is exactly what that means." He

reached down and slipped his hand in hers, then guided her around the front of the horses and took her back several steps, far enough that she could take in the scene.

The horses definitely looked different close up than they did from this distance. The two gorgeous draft horses had been hitched to an old-fashioned sleigh with a spacious curved front and a tall bench seat. The back seat was mostly covered by a lumpy blanket, but a few gifts peeked out from beneath the covering, and the large pine tree they'd originally brought into the barn protruded from the corner at the back. Then, a large hay-style wagon with skis had been attached behind the sleigh and the others were already beginning to climb on board.

"Please tell me we are not going caroling."

"No promises."

Everly wished she had her camera. It was nothing like the monstrosity Penelope used, but it had served her well over the years capturing the places she'd been—not that it had been many.

Oh, wait.

She pulled out her phone and quickly grabbed a shot. A Belgian-pulled sleigh decked out for Christmas in the snow in front of a barn on a ranch. It was the perfect setting for such a night, and she never wanted to forget this moment.

"Come here." Grayson motioned, taking her phone from her. He pulled her in close to his body, his arm wrapped around her, then dropped his head down close to hers, raising the cell above their heads to take a selfie. "Better with us in it, don't you think?" He showed her the screen.

He'd managed to capture the length of the sleigh in the corner of the picture with the ideal backdrop.

"It's perfect," she said, admiring the image before turning to look at him.

When he glanced over, their faces were so close it was almost laughable. He kept his eyes on hers but took a step back.

"Will you send it to me?"

He wants a picture of us. That thought put a little flutter in her gut and she smiled.

"Is that your way of asking for my number?" she teased.

"Yes, ma'am." He was straightforward and direct.

She liked that.

It only took a moment to open a new contact page in her phone.

"Sheriff Grayson Kane," she said as she typed his name, then handed it to him to input the rest of his information.

When he gave it back to her, she saw that he'd modified the name to read, Sheriff Charming. She looked up at him with a raised brow and a dampened smile before sending him a copy of their selfie.

"Done."

"Come on, you guys," someone called from the hay wagon, but it was hard to tell who. "Let's get a move on."

"May I help you up into the Christmas sleigh, ma'am?" His slightly exaggerated drawl evoked a giggle, but she slipped her hand inside of his, and he helped her up into the front seat before striding around to the other side and pulling himself up.

A large fuzzy blanket sat folded on the seat next to her.

"You'll want that," he motioned toward the blanket as he gathered the reins.

Everly opened the thick covering and placed it over her lap, then scooted a little closer to him and extended it over his.

He smiled.

"So, what is Guardian business exactly?" She waited a moment, but when he didn't respond immediately, she followed up. "I mean, I get that you all donate gifts and food to a family that is less fortunate during the holidays, but doesn't everyone do that? Why do you call it Guardian business? Or a Guardian Run?"

"Magic."

"Excuse me?"

"You heard me. Magic. We're not exactly sure which of my relatives started it. It's rumored to be my fifth great-granddaddy, Liam Deardon, but Olivia found evidence in research for one of her books that it was actually his son, my," he squinted one eye as if trying to remember, "fifth great-uncle, Gabe Deardon, in Montana. You should have her tell you the story sometime. Either way, the traditions that come with being a 'Guardian of Christmas Spirit', have been passed down for more than six generations. It's not just about fulfilling a need at Christmastime—which we do—but it's also about keeping the magic of Christmas alive during the season. It brings hope and answered prayers to the folks around here who need it the most."

"Is it just your family?"

Grayson looked over at her for a moment. "You realize that you are sworn to secrecy about all of this."

"Oh, yes. Olivia and Penelope were quite clear about that fact."

"Good."

Dimples.

He brought the sleigh to a stop and handed her the reins.

"What exactly would you like me to do with these?"

If he thinks I'm driving… her thought trailed before it finished.

He pulled a unique, antique-looking lighter from a compartment in the front panel and proceeded to light the lanterns on either side of the sleigh.

"Those are for ambiance," he said as he sat back down. "And this," he pushed a button that turned on what appeared to be electric lanterns that served as headlights on either side of the horses at the front, "is for safety and convenience."

"Convenient." She laughed when they said the words over each other.

"So, Albuquerque," he started, "I need to talk to you."

"Well, good for you then that you have my undivided attention for the next…how long is this drive?"

He chuckled.

"Half an hour. Tops." A fleeting expression of concern crossed his face but was quickly replaced with his natural whimsy.

"What would you like to talk about?" she encouraged.

He cranked his head to look at her.

She could see that something was on his mind, but he turned away from her. Then, with a smile that once again highlighted his dimples, he asked simply, "Who are you?"

"Everly Quinn," she was quick to respond.

"No, I know your name, but who are you?"

He thought for a moment.

"When's your birthday?"

She laughed. "October."

"How many siblings?"

"One."

"Work?"

"Between jobs at the moment."

"What is the worst thing you have ever done?"

She laughed as she quickly scrolled through her life to come up with something quippy but to no avail.

"That—" she finally said, "is a conversation for another day."

"All right," he conceded with a nod, adjusting the reins in his hands.

"Favorite food?"

"That depends on the time of year. Right now, open-face turkey sandwiches smothered in white gravy."

"Nice. And the rest of the year?"

"I like Spanish food."

"You mean like beans and rice?"

"No, I mean like Tortilla de Patata or Bocadillos de Calamares." Just the thought of those two dishes right now had her mouth watering.

"Listen to you. Do you speak Spanish?"

"Si," she said, trying to sound confident. "Una tortilla de patata y un bocadillo de calamares, por favor."

Grayson shook his head and scrunched his shoulders.

"No, I don't speak Spanish. Well, does high school Spanish count?"

"Only if you remember it."

"So, no."

They both laughed.

"How did you learn about those dishes?"

"We were on set with clients in a little town called San Sebastian on the south-eastern coast of the Bay of Biscay in northern Spain. There is a little café there where I stopped almost every day for two weeks and indulged in their delicious foods."

"Spain, huh? Wow, you are a regular world traveler. Maybe I can't call you Albuquerque anymore."

"It was business," she said, remembering the trip all too vividly.

It was the first trip she'd taken after Eli had broken off their engagement and she'd not been in the right frame of mind to take advantage of the opportunity. She shook her head, not caring to remember. "I don't think that counts, but I would love to return there someday as a 'world traveler,' as you say.'"

A moment of silence passed between them.

"Your turn," she said, leaning forward on the seat.

"I suppose that's only fair."

"Okay, um, favorite author?"

"Olivia," he said as if it was a no-brainer.

Everly giggled. She loved that a full-grown man could admit proudly to enjoying a good romance novel.

"Food?"

"Yes." He looked at her with a shrug and chuckled.

"Girlfriends?"

"Working on it," he said with a wink.

"What about Rachel?"

He dropped his head. "You picked up on that, did you?"

"Your mother helped fill in some of the details."

"I'll bet she did. Rachel…is a part of my past."

"Good answer." Everly bumped him with her shoulder. That was all she needed to know on the subject. "Hobbies?"

"It's a little embarrassing, but I like to create pebble art."

"Tell me about that."

"I didn't used to think there was an artist inside of me," he said matter-of-factly. "Always thought that was Landon's area of expertise, but there was this tradeshow that came through a few years ago. I was intrigued by an older gentleman who had created some of the most stunning pieces of art using rocks. Plain, simple, nature-found rocks, pebbles really. Some of his pieces were simple, utilizing a single stone or two with well-placed ink to make up some of the details, and others were masterpieces of carefully selected shapes, colors, and textures that were brought together to create something…" he raised a shoulder in a sort of half-shrug, "that spoke to me. He agreed to teach me, and I've been doing it ever since."

"I'd love to see some of your work."

"I'd love to show you." He reached over and briefly squeezed her hand.

His vulnerability both surprised and touched her, and she wanted to know more.

"So, what made you want to be a sheriff?"

"That's easy. Granddad will tell you that there is an itch in every generation in our family. And maybe that is true, but for me, it's all about helping people in trouble, knowing I made a difference."

"Like you did with me."

He turned to look at her, but in the growing darkness, it was difficult to make out his eyes.

"We're here." Grayson pulled the sleigh to a stop in front of a fairly good-sized log house a way off the beaten road. A flicker of light illuminated a dilapidated railing and several crooked stairs.

She found herself a little disappointed that their conversation had to end, but the anticipation of being a part of something magical excited her.

"Mama arranged for the family to be away from the house for just over an hour tonight, so we'll have to make quick work of it." He jumped down from the seat and hurried over to help her down. "Welcome to the Guardians," he said before joining the others at the back of the sleigh.

Moments later, several large lights had been placed strategically around the front of the house. Landon and Grayson both grabbed shovels and made quick work of clearing a pathway up to the house. Ian and Ben swept off the railing, then carried several long boards up to the stairs and got to work on repairs. Holden carried what looked like a framed door up to the porch.

Olivia stacked a box of supplies along with several gifts into Everly's arms.

"We need to haul all of this up to the porch and arrange it all pretty like," she directed.

After several trips, all the gifts and decorations were ready to be laid out, and Everly was shocked to see that the railing had already been repaired, the new front door had been installed, and a stack of wood had been chopped and placed in a neat pile at the far end of the porch deck.

Grayson and a man she'd never seen before carted the large Christmas tree up onto the porch. The pointed bud at the top of the pine scraped against the overhang, so they leaned it slightly up against the side of the door.

"Everly," Olivia said, "this is the ever-so-handsome Wesley Redbourne. He's one of Grayson's deputies. His daddy is Cass's brother, Thaddeus—Tad for short, and they just live up the street at the SilverHawk."

"It's very nice to meet you, Mr. Redbourne," Everly said, noting the similarities in stature and features with the Kane brothers—though she believed he looked more like Holden than any of them.

"Pleasure's all mine, ma'am. And it's Wes, please."

And charm more akin to Grayson.

She nodded her agreement.

"If you don't mind me saying so, ma'am, you look awfully familiar to me. Have we met somewhere before?"

Everly did not miss the look that transpired between Grayson and his cousin. She scrunched her brows, then raised one as she caught Grayson's eye. He smiled.

"You seem like you would be a hard person to forget, Mr. Redbourne."

He raised a finger to protest.

"Wes," she corrected. "Have you ever been to Albuquerque?"

"Can't say as I have, but...Albuquerque? Isn't that where that fella is from that's coming in for the festival tomorrow?"

She didn't know what to say. She'd nearly forgotten that Eli was coming.

"Wesley," Grayson called out, "we have work to do. Quit your jabbering, would you, and come and hold this up for me please."

"Sorry. Gotta run."

A part of her wanted the snow to start up again so the festival would have to be canceled, but after seeing how hard everyone had worked on the preparations, she recognized that thought to be very selfish. Maybe she could just feign an illness or catch a bus and finally head up to Estes Park to be with her sister. The problem was, Silver Falls had already grown on her, or more importantly, the people. She knew she'd have to leave soon enough and just wanted to enjoy her time with them while she had it.

Penelope pulled out her camera, and while the women worked on staging the gifts and boxes of food and other goodies, and the men hung strands of sparkly lights on the eaves, she snapped pictures.

Everything seemed to be falling right into place. Holden had noticed that the porch swing had come apart but found he had just the right tool to fix it in his box.

Magic.

Wesley happened to have some safety pins in his pocket that secured one of the falling bows to the large garland above the window, and they'd even found a working electrical outlet on the outside of the home.

Magic.

Wreaths, bows, presents, the tree. In minutes everything had been laid out almost like Santa himself had visited the Gusterson's home. And in the evening's light, it almost looked like a scene from a Christmas postcard.

Cass's phone rang.

"All right, Guardians. Our time's up."

Almost as fast as they had put everything up, they had taken down the construction flood lights and the ladders and had packed their tools into the back of the sleigh before jumping up onto the hay wagon. The excited tension in the air was palpable.

Grayson helped Everly up onto the seat and jumped up behind her, sliding her across the seat with his hip as he sat down.

She giggled.

"Gee up," Grayson said softly with a click of his tongue, and the horses turned around under his expert direction. He pulled up behind a tree line, stopped, and cut the lights.

"What are you doing? They'll see us," she said in an instinctual whisper.

Grayson put a finger to his lips. "This is the best part."

Everly looked over her shoulder to see the others all at the

edge of the wagon peering through the obscurity of the trees
and darkness at the beautifully lit scene. It didn't take long
before a large truck pulled up to the house and a little family of
four all climbed down and made their way to the front of the
house. A father with one child in his arms, another hanging
onto his hand, and a woman who appeared to be pregnant
beyond her time.

The father dropped to his knees in the freshly shoveled
snow, releasing his children to rush the porch with squeals of
delight. He dropped his head. His wife placed one hand on the
back of his neck and another across her mouth. She spun
around, searching into the darkness.

The man reached up and took his wife by the hand. It was
impossible to hear what he was saying, but Everly could almost
hear his expressions of gratitude and awe. She found tears
running down her face as she continued to watch the tender
scene.

Grayson had turned sideways on the seat and held open
the blanket, inviting her to sit in the warmth of his embrace.
He pulled her backward and wrapped the covering around her,
holding her close to him. It only took a moment for her to
allow herself to sink into his chest and lean against his neck.

Several minutes passed before the little family had taken
everything inside and it was now safe to leave. Grayson shifted
on the seat, cold air consuming the space he'd just vacated, as
he motioned to the others it was time to go. He turned on the
lanterns, then picked up the reins.

Everly stood up to free the blanket from her backside just
as Grayson clicked his tongue. A light squeal escaped her lips
as she struggled to keep herself upright and regain her balance
when the sleigh jolted into motion.

"Whoa," Grayson said as he jerked on the reins, abruptly
bringing the sleigh to a halt.

Everly fell backward, landing directly on his lap and
leaning backward as if being dipped in a dance, his arms now

surrounding her, a relieved smile gracing his features.

"I'll bet those dimples get you out of just about anything, don't they?" she asked, then groaned inwardly when she recognized her sleepiness symptoms. "Sorry, I didn't mean to say that out loud."

He laughed a little too loudly for their location. "Oh, but you did," he said, helping her back to her place on the bench seat. He tucked the blanket around her, pulling her up close to him as he extended it again across his lap.

They had been traveling for some time when Grayson broke the silence.

"You are something else, Everly Quinn from Albuquerque, you know that? You're funny and kind, and you say what is on your mind even when it could be potentially embarrassing. It's not often I meet a woman like you." He paused a moment. "I've never…actually met a woman quite like you."

What was she supposed to say in response to something like that?

"You know, I'm not always like that. I tend to lose a good portion of my filter when I'm tired. Hopefully, I haven't said anything too embarrassing."

"On the contrary, you told me I'm charming."

She could hear the smile in his voice, and that brought a smile of her own.

"Of course, I did." She slipped her arm into his, and at some point during the short trip, laid her head down onto his shoulder as they passed the remainder of their drive to the ranch in a comfortable silence. By the time they pulled up in front of the barn, tiny crystal snowflakes had begun to dance in the moonlight.

While everyone filed out of the hay wagon, Olivia snuggled into Holden's arm, and Landon and Penelope huddled close together as they approached the sleigh laughing and flirting with one another. It had been a long time since

Everly had been around people with healthy, love-filled relationships. It was refreshing.

"So, how was your first experience as a Guardian?" Penelope asked.

"Does this feeling ever get old?" Warmth still radiated outward from a center mass deep in her chest. If a glow of light had a feeling, this was it.

Almost in unison, she was greeted with a resounding, "Never."

Cass, Ben, and Ian waved goodbye for the night as they trudged through some of the new snow up to the main house.

"It is getting pretty late," Holden said. "And if this weather holds, we'll all be setting up for the festival first thing in the a.m."

"Did you really just say, 'in the a.m.'?" Olivia teased her husband.

"Yes, ma'am." He turned to his brother. "Why don't you two carry on that conversation inside where it's warm? I've got to get these horses brushed down, fed, and watered for the night. My bed is calling my name."

Everly had heard that ranchers went to bed and arose early, but she didn't realize that nine o'clock in the evening was considered late.

"I'll get the hay wagon and sleigh stored up for the night," Landon offered.

Grayson jumped down from the sleigh and held up his arms to help her down, but this time, there were no lingering touches, no intense meeting of the eyes. He simply set her on the ground.

"Everly, there's something I need to talk to you about. And I'm afraid it can't wait." He turned to his sister-in-law. "Liv, could you stick around for a bit?"

She glanced over at Olivia, but it didn't seem the woman knew any more than she did about what was happening. Why would he need Olivia there to talk to her?

Her mind raced.

"Is Violet all right?" It was worry for her sister that had brought her all the way up here to Colorado to begin with.

"I'm sure your sister is fine," Grayson tried to reassure her, "but you're welcome to call her if it would make you more comfortable."

"So, if it's not Violet, what is it that you're not telling me?"

Wes and Grayson exchanged looks again.

"There it is again," she said with a finger pointed at the both of them.

"What?"

"That look between the two of you. I saw it back at that house, but I thought maybe I was just seeing things, but you did it again. Just now. What is that look?"

"It's cold out here," Grayson said as he reached down to take her hand, but she shrugged it off. "Will you come inside with me, please?"

The familiar feeling of dread, like the rug was about to be yanked out from beneath her feet, settled in Everly's belly.

"We'll get ourselves a nice cup of cocoa. With peppermint," Grayson added, tilting his head and smiling as if attempting to coax a smile out of her.

He looked over at Wesley and gestured toward the garage, as he placed a hand in the small of her back to guide her inside. He tugged a single side of the barn doors open and waited for her to go in first.

"I really think we need to build you a regular door into this place, Liv."

Olivia pointed to a regular-sized door that led directly into the office on the other side of the entry.

"Can I get you ladies something to drink?"

"I'm good." She'd trusted him so far, so why did she suddenly feel like a child who'd just gotten into trouble for something she didn't do?

Grayson pointed at the couch with an open palm.

Why was he being so formal all of a sudden?

Everly narrowed her eyes at him, but she stepped inside the now-open barn doors, dragged the beanie from her head, and clutched it in her hands as she took a seat on the couch, both feet on the ground, and her hands in her lap.

Had her instincts been that far off their mark? This had to have something to do with the call he'd received earlier. The mechanic shop.

"How's Frank?" she asked, not wanting to wait until he was ready to deliver his punch line.

The look on his face told her everything she needed to know at that moment.

How could I have been so stupid?

She'd known from the beginning that all of this had seemed too good to be true, but she'd wanted it to be true. Needed it to be true.

But that doesn't make it true, Ev!

Walls that had been melting since she'd arrived in Silver Falls iced over in an instant, and apprehension returned like a familiar companion.

"What can I do for you, *Sheriff?*"

CHAPTER ELEVEN

Grayson knew her use of his title in place of his name shouldn't hurt, but it injured him more than he cared to admit.

"Frank is still in surgery. We won't know for another couple of hours."

"I'm sorry to hear that."

The picture of Everly sitting on the arm of that arrogant writer popped into his head.

"Are you engaged?" he blurted before he could think better of it. It came out almost like an accusation and he knew better, but stood his ground, waiting for an answer.

Everly stared at him. Her eyes narrowed, then her gaze dropped to the ground in front of her, and a little ripple appeared on her jaw and her lips pursed.

"No."

"What is your relationship to Eli Thomas?"

"Is this…? Are you interrogating me?" She took a deep breath and closed her eyes.

"I'd just like to know…*we'd* just like to know," he corrected, "how you know Eli Thomas. Yes, the writer who is coming to Silver Falls."

It took a moment for her to respond, but she opened her eyes again and looked at him. "He *was* my fiancé. Why?"

You are walking on very thin ice, Kane, Grayson warned himself. *Tread lightly.*

He glanced over at Livvy, who sat shaking her head as if to say, 'You're blowing it, Grayson.'

"Was?" Grayson prodded at her use of the past tense. He had to know and couldn't help but feel encouraged by that one little singular word.

"Sorry, *Sheriff*, but I fail to understand what my personal life has to do with your investigation."

Grayson didn't generally consider himself to be the jealous sort, but he couldn't get that photograph out of his head. There had been something about seeing her in another man's arms that had gotten under his skin. They'd had a connection. She'd felt it too, he was sure of it. So, he'd laid it on thick during the Guardian run to see how she would react, and every indication was that she felt the same way.

"If you'd wanted to know about Eli," Everly said quietly, "all you had to do was ask. There are even several very public articles on the subject still available on the internet if you'd like to take just five minutes to look it up." It was the first time he'd seen hurt in her eyes and it pained him to know he'd been the cause. "Go on, I'll wait."

Good to know.

But for the moment, with his personal curiosity satisfied, he could focus on the investigation. The bottom line was, there had been a break-in, and a man was in the hospital fighting for his life. In his experience, old junkers like Everly's were not generally the type of vehicles to be targeted during a break-in, so he had to ask himself, why hers?

He didn't budge.

"How did you know about Eli anyway…" her voice trailed as Wes returned with her box in tow.

He scraped the barn doors closed and walked over to join

them.

"Liv, you really should think about adding an easier entrance to this place," Wes called out casually.

Grayson, Everly, and Olivia all pointed to the office.

"Oh." He set the box down on the coffee table in front of Everly.

"What's this?" she asked, pulling a stapler from her box. "I mean, I know *what* it is, just not why it's here." Her brows scrunched and her eyes flicked between him and Wesley, begging for answers.

"Everly," he tried again, this time the focus on the investigation, "the break-in at the mechanic shop wasn't random. Your vehicle was targeted for a reason, and I need to find out why."

"And you think that Eli had something to do with that? How would he even know where I am? I haven't spoken to the man in months."

Grayson found himself heartened by this revelation.

"No. We don't think Mr. Thomas has anything to do with it—"

"Surely, you don't think *I* had something to do with it?"

"Of course not." This was starting to get out of hand. *Rein it in, Kane.*

"Well, then, help me understand what is happening right now then, Grayson."

His heart flipped a little at the returned use of his given name.

"—but we can't rule *anyone* out until I ask you some questions."

"Why would anyone want to search my truck?" She stood up and started pulling things from the box.

He loved that she still referred to her little matchbox as a truck.

"These are just a bunch of old office supplies and awards from my previous job." She picked up one of the acrylic plaques. "I don't why I even took them really, but why would anyone else want them?" She tossed it back into the box and started to pace in front of the fireplace.

"That is what we were hoping you would tell us." Grayson recognized that having both he and Wes there along with Olivia may not have been the best strategy for getting Everly to open up. He wasn't even sure what he was expecting to discover by talking to her.

"There's nothing to tell." She raised her hands in front of her.

"If you'll just sit back down a moment, Albuquerque, we'll try to get through it as painlessly as possible." He hoped that using his nickname for her would lighten the mood a little.

"Grayson, honey," Olivia said, "why don't you go get Everly a glass of water?"

"I'll get it," Wes volunteered and hopped up to go to the kitchen.

Grayson nodded his appreciation.

"I'd prefer to stand, if it's all the same to you," Everly said, finally meeting his eyes. But the glint of defiance he saw there told him this night was going to get a lot worse before it got any better.

"Fine. Why don't you share with us how you found yourself in the middle of a blizzard so far from home without so much as a coat, yet you have a box full of office supplies from your previous employment. How long have you been in between jobs?" he asked, using her words from the ride earlier that evening.

"Why is this starting to feel more like you are investigating *me* for some wild heist, like robbing a bank or stealing some precious diamond or something? Like I just had it all tucked away in my box of personal belongings, waiting for the exact right moment for a random truck to run me off the road and into a snowbank with no coat, a dead phone, and no plan to speak of?"

Did the woman breathe?

"I thought you were called in to investigate a break-in at the mechanic shop. I have a pretty good alibi for the time it happened." She motioned to Olivia.

"Did you?"

"Did I what? Bludgeon your friend?" She scoffed. "No."

"Rob a bank or steal some precious diamond?"

He didn't believe for one second that she had done either of those things, but the more she made these wildly improbable claims, the more questions arose, and the further they strayed from understanding what had actually happened.

"You got me," she said, throwing her hands madly into the air, then started to pace the room again. "I used my wiles," she stopped and brushed her hands through the air around her very feminine form, "to charm the local sheriff into using his phone to call my partner in crime to come through a blizzard, break into a mechanic shop, bludgeon the mechanic, and take the diamond for safekeeping."

"I should invite you over during my next planning session," Olivia said appreciatively, "I could use ideas like these."

Grayson knew his sister-in-law's comments were in jest, but a part of him believed that Everly could do whatever she put her mind to, and if she'd had a mind to rob a bank or steal a diamond, she could probably do it—especially if she was in cahoots with his sister-in-law.

He raised a brow and Olivia sat back against the couch.

"I don't think you're a jewel thief, Albuquerque. Or a bank robber. But you are giving off a lot of mixed signals here. It's vital for us to get to the bottom of the break-in at the shop and understand why your truck was targeted. We just need you to help us clear things up."

"I don't think anyone is investigating you, Everly. Right, Gray? No one is investigating Everly?"

"No one is accusing her of anything. I'd just like to find out what's happened here. And why? It feels like we are missing something," Grayson picked up the box and carefully dumped its contents onto the coffee table, spreading it out for Everly to see. "This is my town, and I have sworn to protect it. If I have to ask a few uncomfortable questions to get there, that's my job. And it's not always easy."

"So, you *are* investigating me. Do I need my lawyer?" Everly stopped and narrowed her eyes at him.

He reminded himself to keep his voice calm and even.

"Did you find any evidence at all of the person who did this or are you just grabbing at straws?"

"Blood."

"Excuse me?"

"We found blood at the scene that doesn't seem to be Frank's. It'll take a bit to get it analyzed, but until then, we have to do things the old-fashioned way…by asking questions. So, sit!" He was no longer feeling playful, but even then, it came out more firmly than he'd intended, so he added a softer, "Please."

She sat.

"Just take a look through these things, Everly. Did anyone else know you had that box with you? Who knew you were coming to Silver Falls? Was there anything in there of value? Are you missing anything?" While his voice remained even keeled, he hadn't given her a moment between questions to answer anything. He was a better investigator than that and wasn't proud of the way he was handling things. So, he dropped his head and with a deep breath started again. "Everly—"

"Everyone I worked with knew I had that box with me," she cut him off and shot to her feet again. "No one knew I was coming to Silver Falls, including me, because I was headed to Estes Park," her voice was growing louder, her hands flailing about as she paced back and forth in short distances in a monologued response. "There was nothing of any monetary value in there—unless you count the two tickets Mr. Montgomery himself gave me to attend the Montgomery Charity Ball on New Year's Eve in Santa Fe. I believe entrance is upwards of five thousand dollars a plate. And," she bent down to the table and picked up the tickets, "no, I am not missing anything." She threw them back down on the table. "Did *I* miss anything?"

Wes returned with a glass of water.

"I think you've answered all of my questions."

"Wait, all these questions—how could I be so stupid?" She shook her head and took the glass from Wesley. "When's your birthday? you asked. How many siblings? you asked. Work? What's the worst thing you've ever done?" Everly threw her arms up in the air. "Well, it wasn't rob a bank."

It wasn't hard to see how the questions he'd asked her on their ride could have seemed like a covert investigation, but he'd truly wanted to get to know her better. But now, it would be difficult to convince her otherwise.

"I thought you were sweet and genuine, trying to get to know me. That you'd felt the connection between us too, but this whole time," she stopped moving and stood up tall, meeting his eyes, "this whole time, you've just been doing your job." She scoffed again. "I feel so stupid."

Grayson prepared himself for a glass of water to the face, but she closed her eyes and turned around to face the fireplace.

"Look, I know you're upset, and I'm sorry you feel like my questions weren't genuine, but right now, my role is sheriff, and I will play that part by doing everything in my power to keep you and everyone else in this town safe. Do you understand me?" He stepped toward her and placed a hand on her shoulder.

She shrugged it off. "I'm done here," she said in a defeated tone. "I'm going home." She set the full glass of water back down on the table and headed down the hallway toward her bedroom.

"Stop running, Everly," Grayson called as he ran after her. "Stand up and fight for what you want."

"I'm not running," she said even as she reached for her door.

"Yes, you are." Grayson took her hand in his, willing her to face him. "You've seen a glimpse of what life can be like and it scares you because it's different from anything else you've ever known. But different isn't bad, Everly. It's just...different."

She raised her eyes to meet his, defiance burning bright.

"Let go of me." Had she yelled the words in his face, they couldn't have sounded louder in his ears than the deflated whisper of the plea that escaped her lips.

He dropped her hand but couldn't move.

"I can't. My heart won't let me."

He was a man about to lose everything he'd never had a chance to have. His chest constricted, already aching from its loss, and he watched as the fire fizzled out of her.

"You are very good at your job, Sheriff. I have felt safe. Here. With you. And protected. And I even believed that maybe I was ready to do this again. But maybe I was never meant to have all this—whatever this is."

"Don't do that," Grayson said. "Stop pretending that *this* happens every day. You know as well as I do that we've found something real here." He closed the distance between them, placing his hands at her waist from behind, and he leaned down to whisper in her ear. "Something great."

She turned to face him.

"I guess we'll never know."

His heart fell.

"Don't say that."

She placed a hand on his chest just below his shirt collar and played with the buttons there.

He reached up to encase it in his own.

"Thank you for saving me from a miserable and potentially deadly night in the storm." Her voice was chillingly quiet. "Thank you both," she glanced over at Olivia, "for allowing me to participate in your Christmas traditions and giving me such a magical place to stay. It really is beautiful here." Her gaze scanned the room before settling back on Grayson. She smiled softly.

"Then stay," he whispered, wanting desperately just to pull her into his arms. "With me. We'll figure all this out."

Everly took a step back away from him, her hand dropped to her side, and she cleared her throat. "I'll write up a statement today if that's what you need. I've played house long enough. This is not my world. I need to go home, to get back to reality."

"But you said it yourself, there is nothing left for you there. What is it that you want to go back to?"

"I don't know. But it's time to figure it out." She pushed open the door and stood behind it, her face now the only part of her visible to him.

"You don't have to figure it all out alone."

"Goodnight, Sheriff," she said as she closed the door behind her.

Grayson leaned against the frame, his arm above the door and his head low.

"For the record," he said loudly through the wood standing between them, "I had a lot of fun with you today, Albuquerque." As much as his heart was hurting right now, there was still a job to do. "But the fact remains…someone broke into your truck and tossed through that box looking for something. You may be the only one who can help us find out why Frank is in the hospital and if someone dangerous is still on the streets in Silver Falls." He waited a moment with no response. "Everly?"

If the culprit had gotten what he'd come for, he would be long gone from their little town, but if he hadn't, Everly and anyone who associated with her could be in danger.

He stood there for what felt like an eternity before he turned around and slid to the floor, extended his legs out in front of him, and leaned against the door frame. He couldn't let her leave. Not like this.

"Gray," Olivia sat down on the floor with her legs crossed in front of him.

"She's the one, Liv."

"I know."

CHAPTER TWELVE

Everly pulled back the sheer white curtains in her room and glanced out the window at the fresh morning snow. The storm had finally passed, which meant that the Silver Falls Festival would likely proceed as originally planned. She glanced down at her watch.

Nearly five-thirty.

She'd spent most of the night tossing and turning, crying, and pounding on her poor, beautifully wonderful pillow trying to figure out how last night had gone so wrong. Admittedly, she'd been hurt to find out that Grayson's attempts at getting to know her had not been solely based on a mutually-shared, genuine interest, but were a part of his investigation—especially because she had already fallen for him, despite her best intentions.

But at some point during the night, she'd allowed his words to really sink in and understand where he'd been coming from. She'd been too quick to jump to conclusions, to discount his intentions, and it hadn't looked pretty.

It was early enough that she hoped she would be able to catch everyone before they left for town. She slipped into the jeans that Penelope had lent her and Olivia's cranberry scoop neck sweater with the lantern sleeves and buttons trailing the arm seams. She wished she had time to make Grayson some apology German pancakes and bacon this morning to help ease the awkwardness from her childish outburst last night. He likely would never want to speak to her again, but she had to try.

Everly brushed through her hair, surprised it had retained some of its curl, then she brushed her teeth and applied a fresh coat of mascara and lip balm before heading out to the living room. She stopped short when she saw Grayson standing with his back to her, his hands in his pockets as he stared down into the flames of the large electric fireplace. She would have expected him to be in flannel and denim for the day, but he was still dressed in the same champagne button-down shirt with rolled sleeves and dark slacks from the night before, and she took a moment to appreciate his toned physique from afar.

He was a beautiful man.

Had she known he was going to stay in the barn all night, she would have cleared her conscience with him hours earlier.

"Good morning," she said, hating to interrupt his thoughts.

"You're up early," he responded without looking at her.

"Barely slept if I'm being honest."

He turned just enough that she could see half of his face.

"Me neither," he said with a smile just wide enough to show the beginnings of his dimple.

"Can we talk?" she asked, taking a step toward him.

Grayson nodded once, then moved over to the couch and sat down without looking at her. He leaned forward, his forearms resting on his thighs and his hands folded together, still facing the fire.

Everly sat down next to him, resting her leg lightly against his.

How do I start?

"I'm sorry." There was more to say, but that was the most important. She paused, placing a hand on his exposed forearm. "There are a lot of reasons for what happened last night, but none of them excuse the way I acted."

He looked down at her touch, then reached over and gently traced the contours on the back of her hand with his thumb.

"I understand that you were only trying to do your job," she continued. "And I know that there is something…special…between us."

He enclosed the whole of her hand in his, then turned to look at her.

"Truth is, you were right," she breathed a laugh, not quite ready to meet his eyes. "I'm scared. I'm scared of trusting my instincts again. I'm scared of change. I'm scared that my feelings for you have grown so quickly. And I'm scared of losing you." She laughed uneasily. "I know what that must sound like." She mustered the courage to lift her gaze and felt a new wave of butterflies fluttering in her belly when her eyes met his. "I haven't felt this alive in—"

Grayson bent toward her, claiming her lips in a kiss.

A surge of emotion exploded inside of her, nerve endings suddenly ablaze beneath his touch, but with more restraint than she could have known herself capable, Everly pulled back just far enough that she could speak. She had to know.

"Are you sure this is what you want, Gray? That I…am what you want?"

He released his grip on her hand and moved his to the side of her face, his thumb caressing the edge of her chin.

"You," he brushed the tip of her nose with his and leaned in again, taunting her with the nearness of his lips, his warm, minty breath mingling with her own, "are exactly what I want. *Who* I want."

He kissed her once more, melting the wall that she had put up between them. But one question still burned in her mind. She wrapped her fingers around his wrist and broke away ever so slightly.

"How do you know?"

Grayson pulled back just enough to meet her eyes. "Because my heart recognized yours as its missing piece the moment you fell into my arms."

He didn't move but held her gaze, his thumb brushing across her chin until his hand rested at the side of her neck.

She knew she was his. No questions lingered, and she reached up, her fingers nesting at his nape as she leaned forward, drawing him back toward her until their lips met again in a light kiss, and another, deepening as she tilted her head to the other side and surrendered to the unspoken promise it held. At that moment, she was exactly where she belonged.

When their kiss broke, they leaned back against the back of the couch, and Everly rested her head in the crook of Grayson's neck, his arms wrapped around her, holding her close. He kissed her temple, then nestled his cheek against her head.

She smiled softly, savoring the moment that would be engraved on her heart forever.

With very little sleep, Everly's eyelids grew heavy and threatened to close. She allowed herself to indulge in the comfort of being nestled beside him for only a few moments before forcing herself from the warmth of Grayson's arms and sitting upright on the couch.

His eyes were still closed. The growing smile on his face did nothing to prepare her for him to launch upright, scoop her in the crook of his arm, and pull her back into his embrace.

"What time are you supposed to be meeting your mother?" Everly asked, still laughing as she glanced up at the hands of the clock on the wall.

"Right now," he said matter-of-factly, but making no effort to move.

The flash drive.

Everly bolted out of his arms.

"Oh, I almost forgot." She sprung to her feet and pulled her phone from her back pocket, opened the purple embossed case, and retrieved a thin black and red flash drive.

In the middle of the night, as she'd gone over in her head everything that had happened when she left R&J, she remembered the drive. She held it out for him.

He reached up and took it from her. "What's this?"

She tucked one leg underneath her and sat down on the couch to face him, then took a deep breath.

"So," she started, not really wanting to relive the day, but knowing it might be what he needed, "the day we met, I'd just been fired from my position at R&J because they'd brought in a new management team, and the man assigned to be my new boss is a slimeball who can't keep his hands to himself. He is unaccustomed to strong women who aren't afraid to tell him no." She'd practiced this speech too many times last night and hoped she didn't sound like a fool.

She glanced down as his hand closed into a fist, but he said nothing, just bobbed his head, encouraging her to go on.

"Before I left his office," she continued. "I swiped that little drive containing my portfolio and campaign ideas off his desk, gathered the rest of the things from mine, put them all into that box, and walked out of the office."

Grayson placed his hand on her forearm but still said nothing.

"When I got out to my truck, my brother-in-law called to tell me that Violet, my sister who is very, very pregnant by the way, had been in an accident." She shrugged. "So, I left. Without stopping at home. Without so much as a word to anyone. I didn't think about it, I just…left."

Grayson shifted on the couch so he could look at her directly.

"That's a lot of stress for one day."

"Tell me about it." She tried to brush the all-too-recent memories aside, but she was grateful that he seemed to understand.

"I'm so sorry that happened to you."

"Thank you." She squeezed his arm.

"And then to be involved in your own accident that night, stranded with a bunch of Christmas-crazy strangers, and—"

"Finding you?"

"Okay, maybe it wasn't all so bad," he teased, his face brightening with a smile.

"It wasn't until I picked up my phone last night to check what time it was that I remembered the drive. I doubt it's anything, but I want to help you find whoever hurt your friend however I can. And if you think that something on my portfolio might help, then it's yours."

"Thank *you*...for this," Grayson said sincerely, his smile fading slightly as he held up the flash drive. "I know it's been hard, especially after the last couple of days, but the faster we can figure out why Frank is in the hospital and why we have someone dangerous lurking around Silver Falls, especially during the festival, the better off we'll all be."

He jumped up off the couch and held his hand out to help her up. When she slipped her hand into his, he pulled her into his arms.

"And I'm sorry about Eli."

"I'm not. His choice is ultimately what brought me here to Silver Falls. To you."

The lines around Grayson's eyes crinkled, and he planted a sweet little kiss on her lips as if he'd done it a thousand times.

"Come on, we're going to be late," he said, heading for the doors.

Everly grazed her fingers over her lips, still tingling from his kisses, and followed.

"Exactly where I belong," she whispered to herself.

It was still dark outside when they left the warmth of the

barn. A large black truck rumbled, and the exhaust looked like waves of rolling clouds coming in. Olivia climbed down out of the truck and rushed over, beaming at them.

"Does this mean that you're staying?" she asked, clutching Everly's hands in hers.

"I am."

The woman pulled her into a hug. "I'm so glad. You deserve a little happy after everything that you've been through. HEAs shouldn't only be reserved for the characters in romance novels."

Everly scrunched her brows together.

"H.E.A.," Olivia said again as if slowing it down would make it easier to understand. "No?" She shook her head when Everly still looked at her blankly. "Happily. Ever. Afters."

"Ah," Everly said with a laugh.

"I've got a little something for you, but you'll have to stop by my booth later to get it. Okay?"

"Wouldn't miss it."

When the sun finally peeked above the mountaintops and illuminated the town's square, Everly felt like she was on the set of any one of several of her favorite Christmas movies. A large tree stood at the town's center, ornately dressed in large bulbs of bright colors, red bows, and tinsel, and ready for the tree-lighting that would come tomorrow night at the end of the festival. Garlands had been strung across the eaves of the shops that lined the street, and the smells of freshly baked goods and other delectable treats permeated the air around her.

Once the dance hall, vendor booths—which all looked like their own miniature little A-frame cabins complete with heaters inside for the vendors—and food tables had all been set up and decorated, Everly picked up a flyer that contained a map of the entire event from the free-standing pocket shelf just outside the quaint little gazebo in the corner of the square and quickly planned the direction she would follow. Since Grayson would be busy patrolling the area, specifically the art walk where Rachel had requested additional security, she decided that would be as good a place as any to begin.

As she strolled past various art displays, she marveled at the talent, creativity, and individuality of such a wide variety of artistic expressions, still amazed that so many of them had shown up despite the storm that had threatened to cancel the entire event.

The snow-capped mountains and picturesque landscape in one artist's painting in particular resonated with her and she stepped a little closer to examine it further. To her delight, she found a small herd of reindeer depicted in the snowy forest behind a cabin nestled in the woods. She glanced down at the artist's signature, but couldn't quite make it out.

"You like it?"

Warm recognition spread through her chest.

"Nothing surprises me in this little town," Everly said with a grin as she turned around, slipping under Ian's extended arm for a hug. "You're the artist? It looks just like the scene we saw from the balcony in the barn."

"You, little lady, discovered one of my favorite spots to think and paint. You have a good eye."

"May I purchase this one, please? It'll be like having a little piece of home with me wherever I go."

"And are you planning on going somewhere?" The familiar voice brought tears to Everly's eyes.

Violet?

She whipped around and rushed into her very pregnant sister's arms without warning. All of the stresses and worries, joys, and hope that she'd felt over the last couple of days seemed to pour out of her into that single embrace. She had so much to tell her baby sis, so much to share.

Owen scooped them both into a bear hug, evoking teary-eyed giggles.

"What are you doing here, Vi?" Everly pulled back enough to hold both of her sister's shoulders as she drank in the sight of her.

"Do you remember that festival I was telling you about on the phone the other day? Well, this is it. When we got a call from Grayson last night asking us to come, it wasn't hard. We already have reservations at the cutest little inn in town."

"The Snowy Pines Inn?"

"You know it?"

Everly laughed out loud, so excited to have her sister here with her right now.

"Wait, did you say that Grayson called you? Last night?"

He had taken her sister's number in case of an emergency.

"That man loves you, Ev. There is no doubt in my mind."

"He's known me less than forty-eight hours…" But even as she protested, she knew she loved him too.

"Oh, where are my manners?" She took a step back to show the artist.

"This is—"

"Ian Redbourne," Owen said, extending his hand out to Grayson's granddad. "It's good to see you."

Everly shook her head with a laugh. "I was going to say, Theodore Blackwood…"

Ian beamed.

Violet mouthed the name of Olivia Blake's patriarchal character in her Blackwood novels, then opened it with more than a hint of excitement. It was obvious she recognized it.

"…but, how do you two know each other exactly?"

"When one of you runs a ranch and the other is an Environmental Consultant, you tend to run in some of the same circles."

"I'm not really surprised by anything here anymore. Except this," she squeezed Violet again, unable to take her arm from around her baby sister. "This… was a surprise. A wonderful surprise."

She handed Ian the money for the painting, and her eye was drawn to a gentleman in a long, dark overcoat in the next booth seeming to glance over a box of handmade Christmas cards, though the box was upside down.

"Granddad," she turned to Ian, "have you ever seen…" she glanced back up to point out the man, but he was gone.

"Seen what, sis?" he asked, twisting around to follow the direction of her gaze.

"Never mind. It was probably nothing." She smiled. "I wonder if I might arrange to have this beautiful painting delivered," she teased.

"I think we can work something out." He winked at her and reached up to take the painting off the hook at the side of the booth and placed it in a box beneath the table.

She leaned over and kissed the old man on the cheek.

"Thank you, Granddad" she whispered, and he gave her a light squeeze.

This morning her heart felt lighter than it had in a long time. It was like a weight she'd been carrying around with her for the better part of a year had been lifted and she could see things more clearly now. Though it was slightly overshadowed by thoughts of the strange gentleman at the other booth.

Could that have been the man who'd broken into her truck and hurt Frank? She certainly hadn't recognized him, but she made a mental note about everything she remembered about him to offer Grayson when she saw him. She looked over her shoulder and did a quick scan of the booths in her sight. He wasn't there. He'd simply disappeared and that made her a little wary.

Everly wasn't sure who seemed to be enjoying the artist walk of the festival more—Violet or Owen. Her brother-in-law asked each of the different artisans active questions, listened intently to their answers, and tried all the food samples offered to him.

They stopped by the potter's booth and watched as the artist crafted a new functional piece of pottery on his wheel as part of his demonstration. Three large portable heaters had been strategically placed around the platform, likely to keep the man warm while he threw. After a moment of warming herself a little in his space, they moved on.

One shop was filled with handwoven scarves and blankets. Everly ran her hands over the scarf the designer had displayed on a mannequin to the side of his table. She couldn't help but think how good the deep red would look under Grayson's brown suede and shearling coat—and how appropriate for Christmas.

There were so many wonderful artists who had come to share their talents. She realized she needed to slow down her spending, or she would end up panhandling her way back to New Mexico. That thought brought her up short.

No, not New Mexico.

There was nothing for her there anymore. Silver Falls had everything she could ever want.

Except maybe a job, she conceded.

But she would start her own company if necessary. This was where she wanted her life to be. This was home. Because this was where Grayson was.

Everly spotted Penelope and Landon sitting down in front of a vendor booth that had been decked out with garlands and holly strung along the eaves of the tent, and ornaments dangling from the ceiling. Both canvas and framed art prints had been arranged elegantly on black draped walls, on the black cloth-covered table, and in two tall round-turn displays on either side of the booth.

There, on one of the turntable displays, staring back at her was Grayson's face. Everly's eyes widened, and she rushed to the stand, snatching up the calendar that she had heard so much about right off the display. She knew that Landon had done the photography for the charitable calendar and that all three Kane brothers had posed, but she'd had no idea Grayson was the cover. He certainly did it justice.

"Did my little brother tell you that he is Mr. December?" Landon asked with a grin.

"No, but your mother did." She laughed as she flipped through the pages. "Mr. November, I presume," she said as she opened the calendar to the page where Landon posed in front of a beautiful landscape of fall foliage holding his camera.

"You got me."

"And he is a very handsome Mr. November, if I do say so myself." Penelope walked over and placed a light kiss on his cheek. Landon pulled her into his arms, dipped her, and kissed her smack dab on the mouth.

When he lifted her up, Penelope smiled, fanning herself animatedly.

Everyone laughed. Some people from the surrounding areas even clapped.

Everly noted the fresh color that appeared in Penelope's cheeks. After she had introduced her sister and brother-in-law to them, her new friend grabbed her by the arm.

"Did you see that Grayson set up a booth this year?" she asked, motioning to the stall just around the corner from theirs.

Grayson had not said a word about having his own booth for the festival, and Everly wondered when he'd had the time to come set it up. He'd been with her all morning. Well, obviously not all morning if he had a booth set up.

"How?"

"You should go see it. His art has surprised everyone this year."

"Okay, but you know I need this, right?" Everly asked, holding up the calendar. She handed Penelope some cash but refused the change. "It's for a good cause."

The man in the overcoat appeared again at the corner of the arena where they were conducting live food demonstrations. He made eye contact with her as he raised a small plate and took a bite of something.

He's got nerve, I'll give him that.

She thought it was probably time to find Grayson as both of her encounters with this man had left her a little unsettled.

"Violet," she called for her sister. "Do you see that man standing over there by the booth selling schnitzel?"

"Mmmm…they have a booth selling schnitzel? Can we go there next?"

Several groups of people passed by them, but when they cleared, the man was gone. Again.

All the same, Everly turned back to Penelope and Landon and spoke in hushed tones as not to alarm her sister.

"Hey, there's a man walking around in a dark overcoat who's acting…odd." It was as good a word as any. "I have a bad feeling about him and wonder if he might have had something to do with Frank."

"Will do," Landon said, now scanning the town square.

As Everly, Violet, and Owen rounded the corner to visit Grayson's booth, Everly was caught off guard when saw him. Eli Thomas sat behind a large table inside of the largest tent surrounded by fans of all ages clamoring to get a moment of his attention. He was as handsome as ever in his faded green collared jacket and teal Henley shirt that looked really good but wasn't really weather-appropriate.

It appeared as if the author's booths had been collected together in the short, cul-de-sac-style protrusion between the barbershop and the post office that culminated behind Grayson's booth.

Violet tugged on Everly's coat. "Why is Eli here?" she leaned over and asked quietly.

"It's a long story, but apparently, he is friends with a local from college and wanted to write a Christmas children's book about this town." She looked up thoughtfully. "I guess that it's not such a long story."

"You knew he was coming?"

"I learned about it the night I arrived."

"And look," Owen said, "his booth is right next to Olivia Blake."

Her sister bounced a little on her feet and hit Everly's arm with the back of her hand. "Olivia Blake is here."

With everything else that had been going on, Everly couldn't believe that she'd left out the fact that she was now friends with their favorite author.

"I know. Did I neglect to mention that she's Grayson's sister-in-law?"

Violet stopped fan-girling for five seconds, her eyes boring into Everly's and a challenging brow raised. "Are you seriously telling me that the Olivia you have been hanging out with all weekend, whose barn you are staying in, is Olivia Blake?"

"Kane actually," she repeated Olivia's previous correction.

Her sister ignored her. "That was a convenient detail to leave out. The fact that she is practically your sister-in-law."

"Okay, let's not go getting ahead of ourselves here."

"Your comment back there about Theodore Blackwood totally makes more sense now."

"I did tell you that Ian is Grayson's granddad, right?" Everly was almost afraid of the answer.

"Stop it!" Violet said with another smack to Everly's arm.

It was hard to tell if the expression on her face was amusement or bewilderment.

"Who are you, and what have you done with my meticulous, planner of a sister who is never short on detail?"

Everly laughed.

"Hi, Wesley," she said with a wave as she stepped up to the edge of the booth where he stood with his Stetson hat and pine green survival jacket, his deputy badge proudly displayed on his chest. "About last night…"

She definitely had not been at her best.

"Don't think another thing about it." He waved a hand in the air to brush it off as if it had been nothing. "I know it's been rough. Gray told me that you remembered something about a flash drive."

"You are very gracious, and yes, I'd forgotten I'd put my portfolio in my wallet." She held up her phone. "I gave it to him this morning."

Suddenly, the hairs stood up on the back of Everly's neck and she glanced around looking for the man in the overcoat.

"Are you all right?" Wes asked.

"Oh, yes, fine. Sorry." She shook her head. "So, did you draw the short stick? Where's the sheriff?"

"Aunt Cass has actually been running the booth, but I stepped in for her momentarily while she takes care of some "festival business."" The last he said with air quotes.

"I thought Rachel was worried there wouldn't be enough security in this section of the festival, but I haven't seen any officers or deputies. Other than you, of course."

"Turns out, the art walk has been the least of our problems today. Already, there's been a lost child looking for her mother, someone who backed into the festival marquee post, Mathias Richards showed up drunk, a badger decided to join the festivities and was waddling down the center of Main Street, and some teens tried grabbing the cash box from Santa's Village. We've had our hands full."

"I guess that would do it. So," she said as she actually turned to look inside of the booth, "tell me about this pebb..le...art. Wow!" she said, stunned at the scene staring back at her.

Perched on an easel behind the front table sat a beautifully intricate square piece of framed pebble artwork she guessed to measure at least twenty-four inches in diameter. Stones of all shapes and sizes had been pulled together to create the most intricate designs that resembled the ebb and flow of flowing water. Swirls of pebbles with similar shapes and sizes were grouped together emanating from the central mound of larger stones.

"It's beautiful," Violet echoed her thoughts. "Did you know he could do this?"

"He told me about his art, but I had no idea he could do *this*."

She glanced at several of the other pieces. She'd never seen anything quite like them. Some were more simple, using only a couple of pebbles, while those like the large, framed piece were intricate in design and depth. She couldn't imagine how much some of them probably weighed.

When Grayson had told her that he liked to do pebble art as a hobby, this was nothing like she had imagined. She had mistakenly assumed it would be similar to rock painting—and she'd seen some very unique and incredible painted rocks, but this was definitely not that. Somehow, this fit him.

"My little brother is quite the talent, wouldn't you say?" Holden stood next to her, admiring some of Grayson's pieces.

"I'd say all of you ooze with talent."

He laughed.

"Holden, this is my little sister, Violet, and her husband, Owen." The couple leaned over the front table, gawking at several of the simple framed pieces. They turned around at the mention of their names. Violet held an art piece depicting a romantic couple holding a new baby sitting on a bench under a full moon.

"Isn't it stunning?" she asked, holding it up.

"Yes," Everly breathed, "it's beautiful. Violet, this is Grayson's oldest brother." A part of her wished that all of them were together so she would only have to introduce everyone once.

"You're the architect Ian speaks so highly of," Owen said as he shook Holden's hand.

"I suppose that would be me—especially if you've been talking to my granddad."

"And Olivia Blake's husband," Everly added in for good measure.

Color crept into Violet's cheeks.

"Speaking of talent and my wife," Holden said, his palms together, "she has been trying to get your attention for several minutes now." He pointed over to where Olivia sat with a healthy line of fans waiting to purchase and have her sign their books. "She thinks that maybe you're trying to avoid coming to see her because of who she's been seated next to."

"Really? That doesn't sound like me." Everly smiled. "Tell her we're on our way."

Holden took two steps, then turned around.

"And by 'on your way' you mean…?"

"I mean we're on our way. Now. Well, in like two minutes," she clarified. She still wanted to peruse Grayson's booth, but decided there would be plenty of time to see them later. Now was as good a time as any to put on her big girl panties and face what she'd been avoiding all year. Coming face to face again with Eli.

She threaded her arm through her sisters. "Are you ready?"

"Are you kidding?"

Owen walked with them, Violet's hand snuggly resting inside of his. When they reached Olivia's table, the author glanced at the small group and her face lit up.

"You have to be Violet," she said, making her way around the table to greet them. "Grayson told me you'd be coming to our little festival today, and Everly has told us so much about you. But, I must say, you are even more radiant in person." She opened her arms and pulled Violet in for a hug. "And you," she motioned to Owen, "must be the proud daddy."

"Yes, ma'am. Owen Carter."

As Olivia and the others chatted, Everly saw the man in the overcoat standing just a few feet away on the other side of Eli's booth, half obscured by the tent's rolled sides.

"Will you all excuse me a moment?" she asked, wanting to talk to the man, but not daring to take her eyes off him for fear he'd disappear again.

When the stranger caught her eye, he ducked into the crowd, but this time, without thinking, Everly followed. Her heart pounded in her chest, the crisp air filling her lungs with vigor as she weaved hastily through the bustling street. The boots the girls had lent her gave her good traction, providing a confident grip on the snowy ground as she pursued the stranger.

Past the savory food stalls and warm yeasty aromas coming from the sweet-bread demonstration, past the carolers singing their festive tunes, and past a group of children building snowmen in the square, Everly's breaths came more heavily with each step, but she had to know why the strange man had been following her.

As she rounded the corner of booths vending specialty ornaments and traditional decorations, she came across the overcoat lying in the snow, but the man who'd worn it had disappeared into the crowd of festival visitors. She picked up the garment, her breaths coming out in short, visible puffs of white in the chilly air as she looked from one booth to another, through the crowd and everywhere for some glimpse of someone who didn't belong. Her heart raced as she stood on her tiptoes, scanning the festive snow-covered streets for any sign of the man.

But he was gone.

CHAPTER THIRTEEN

With the dark overcoat in hand, Everly returned to the little author's cove where Olivia and Violet were still deep in conversation.

"Everly?"

She glanced over to see her ex waving at her from behind his table, and she groaned.

Not now. She wasn't ready.

"Eli?" She sorta waved and offered him a half smile.

"Excuse me a moment, would you?" he asked the woman standing in front of his table, then rushed over to greet her.

He stared a moment as if not knowing exactly what to say. A first for him.

"It's been a long time, Eli," she said with a light bob to her head.

"You look great," he offered.

"So do you." They exchanged pleasantries.

Everly waited for the familiar pang of his loss to pierce a dagger through her core like it had every time his name had been mentioned on the TV or at work, but it didn't come. She felt fine. In fact, she felt…nothing.

"What are you doing here, Everly? In Silver Falls? Did you follow me up here? Today, of all days?"

Everly was taken aback by his question. She'd never really stopped to think how it might look that he'd been slated to come to this little town for ages, but she just happened to end up in the exact same place. She had to stop and think.

Today of all days?

She couldn't believe she'd forgotten. She swallowed hard.

Our wedding day.

"Why would I follow you, Eli? I don't need to keep up with your social calendar anymore."

"I don't know, I thought maybe, like me, you've been reminiscing. About us."

"What 'us,' Eli? There hasn't been an 'us' for quite some time."

"Eli, honey," a woman called out to him, placing a hand intimately on his arm, "they are wanting you to—" she stopped short of finishing her sentence when she saw Everly.

"Hello, Sheila," Everly said.

Of course.

Without another thought, Everly started to laugh.

"It all makes sense now," she said as she looked back and forth between Eli and his publicist, who now had slipped one hand into his and the other strategically on the crook of Eli's arm, showing off the diamond on her finger.

Violet and Olivia rushed to Everly's side.

"Miss Quinn," Sheila acknowledged, not as surprised to see her as Everly would have expected. "I was wondering when we might run into you."

"Don't 'Miss Quinn', me, Sheila. We've known each other far too long for that." Everly didn't know what game the woman was playing at, but she didn't like it. "You knew I was here?" she asked.

"I may have seen you earlier," she said with a little shrug, "hanging garlands on the gazebo with the event staff."

Eli took a step back, looking at her with surprise. "And you didn't think to tell me?"

Sheila cocked her head and pouted her lips, pulling him back in close to her, her hand still entwined in his. "Don't hate me for hoping you wouldn't see the ex it took you nearly a year to get over."

Everly was shocked to hear that little tidbit of information. "He broke up with me, remember?"

"Don't you just love this quaint little town and all its charm?" Sheila said as if she hadn't heard Everly's clear reminder of their history. "It has a way of drawing you in when you least expect it." The woman's disingenuous smile stretched her already overly plastic face as she glanced around. "Life has a funny way of working out, doesn't it? I had no idea it was so far up into the mountains. It was hard to get to, but once I got out of the storm, it was worth it."

"Are you staying at the Snowy Pines Inn?" Everly asked.

"We are now," Sheila said with a roll of her eyes. "I've only been here a few days now, and here the past has already resurfaced bringing unwanted…challenges to deal with."

Eli slipped his arm around his fiancée. "After speaking with one of the event coordinators, she decided to come up a day early to vet a couple of alternate locations in case the storm didn't clear up, and ended up having to stay at a little motel across town for the first night."

"It wasn't exactly cozy," Sheila said with a facial sneer.

"The inn is owned by the family of one of my friends from college. She booked me—"

Sheila elbowed him in the side.

"Er, us, rooms months ago."

"Rachel," Everly said without thinking.

"Yes, how did you know?"

"We met the other night," she admitted, kicking herself for mentioning it, "and when she informed me about your new project and that you would be coming, she didn't hesitate to tell me how close the two of you were in college."

"It wasn't like that, Ev."

She put her hand up. "Not my business," she said, shaking her head.

Even though Olivia and Violet remained quietly by her side, Everly was comforted to know she had their support, and they were there if she needed them.

"Eli," Sheila said, glancing down at her watch, "while we all want to hear more about your extensive list of girlfriends, they're waiting for you over by Santa's Village." She started to walk away, pulling him by the hand, then turned and looked at him expectantly.

Everly found the irony in that.

"The reading is about to start," Sheila informed him.

"Well, they can't exactly start without me, now, can they?" he told her with a little laugh. "Will you just go let them know that I'll be a minute?"

Sheila let go of his hand. "Don't be too long," she said, offering a little half-wave at Everly before leaving.

"Be careful in those boots, Sheila," she called after the woman. "They weren't exactly made for these Silver Falls winters. I'd hate to see you fall."

"I wouldn't," Violet whispered behind her.

"I was going to tell you, Ev. Really, I was. About the engagement, I mean."

Her first instinct was to ask him if Sheila was the sort to fit into his image or his bottom line, but she realized it would be petty. That it didn't matter. She didn't care anymore.

"Eli," she said, reaching forward and placing a hand on his arm, "If you are happy with Sheila Reed, I am so happy for you." Some of the awkwardness had lifted between them now that the woman was gone. "Everyone deserves to be happy. And if she makes you happy, then, I'm glad."

He tilted his head, his eyebrows peaked, his eyes wide, and his mouth slightly open.

"Thank you," he said, visibly attempting to shake off his surprise. "Are you?" He cleared his throat. "Happy?"

Everly had to think about his question for a minute.

"You know, life *does* have a funny way of working out. For the first time in nearly a year," she said, images and thoughts of Grayson filling her mind and bringing a smile to her face, "I'm actually feeling really good. I'm hopeful."

"That's really good, Ev. I, uh, have heard that you've been working a lot. Too much even lately."

"Keeping tabs on me?" She didn't know whether to be flattered or insulted.

"No, but we still run in some of the same circles, and I hear things. Like you haven't dated anyone since we broke up. That you've buried yourself with work. And that maybe you'd be open to—"

"There you are, sweetheart."

The sound of Grayson's voice widened the grin on her face and brought a tingling warmth that spread from head to toe.

"I've been looking all over for you." He slipped his arms beneath hers from behind and pulled her back against him, placing his jaw against the side of her head. "I'm so sorry I'm late. We've had several emergencies to deal with this morning." His appearance was an instant infusion of laughter and joy, love, and acceptance—such a stark contrast from what she'd ever felt with Eli. If there had been any doubt in her mind before, there was none now.

Grayson Kane was her person.

If Everly thought Eli had looked surprised before, now he appeared to be stunned speechless.

"Who's your friend?" Grayson asked nonchalantly, playing his role effortlessly.

"Um, *honey*," she wasn't sure what to call him at this point, "this is Eli Thomas. Remember, I told you about him. That we used to date."

Eli cleared his throat and shook his head as if to clear it from the shock, and Everly had to admit she was enjoying it more than a little.

"We were engaged, actually," Eli corrected. "I'm sorry," he asked, looking a little flustered as he turned to Grayson, "but who are you?"

Grayson pulled one of his arms out from beneath hers and extended a hand.

"Sheriff Grayson Kane. Evvie's current and last fiancé."

Evvie? Hmmm, she kind of liked how it sounded coming off his lips, then choked down her own surprise.

"Fiancé?" Eli's eyes shot to Everly, questioning. "You're getting married? When did this happen? I thought you weren't even seeing anyone."

"I'm afraid that's yesterday's news," Grayson said without missing a beat.

Literally.

Everly snorted, which made everyone around them laugh except for Eli.

She could see that he was perplexed, so she took in a breath, willing her pulse to calm.

"It's true," she said, thinking carefully on how to present her next words, "our relationship is fairly new. When you left, I never thought I could love anyone ever again."

I guess we're being vulnerable now. But she didn't stop.

"I thought I was broken, Eli. But Grayson changed that. From the moment we met, he's made me feel special, loved, appreciated, and included. He's not worried about what anyone else thinks. He's seen the not-so-pretty side of me," she squeezed his arms remembering last night's faux paus, "and he loves me anyway."

Eli took a step toward them. "Ev, I—"

She didn't let him speak.

"He's shown me in a short time what it feels like to be free to let my guard down and be loved and needed just for being me. I've never met anyone who makes me laugh the way he does."

"I'm sorry if I ever made you feel like you weren't important to me. You'll always be the one who got away." Eli swallowed, then met her eyes. "So, you're happy then?" he asked again.

"I think for the first time in my life, Eli, I understand that my happiness is no one's responsibility, but my own. But am I happy? Yes. Because I am where I belong."

Grayson squeezed her a little tighter and kissed the top of her head.

"That's good," Eli said, bobbing his head appreciatively. "I should use that in one of my books."

"Already taken," Olivia chimed in.

"All right, well, I guess I am needed in Santa's Village. It really is great to see you, Ev. I'm so happy for you," he echoed her previous sentiments.

"Sheriff…Grayson," he said, extending his hand again. "Keep her safe."

Everly felt the movement of his head and guessed he nodded behind her.

As Eli turned to leave, he glanced back. "And, Ev, for what it's worth…I'm sorry."

Don't cry. Don't cry. Don't cry.

"Thank you."

Everly waited until Eli was out of sight before turning around in Grayson's arms.

"Engaged?"

CHAPTER FOURTEEN

"Did you mean all those things you said or were you just playing a part?" Grayson had a thousand things he was itching to say, but he wanted to make sure he knew where he stood before he said them.

Everly stared up at him, the corners of her mouth twitching upward.

"Sheriff, we have a visual," the voice crackled over Grayson's radio.

HONK! BLARE! WAIL! HONK! BLARE! WAIL!

"Arg. I'm sorry, *sweetheart*, I have to go. That's the alarm on my truck." Grayson dropped his arms from around her but leaned over and placed a light, quick kiss on her lips. "This isn't over," he whispered, reiterating his promise from yesterday.

"Wait. Grayson," she gripped tighter onto his hand and tugged him back to her, then held out a dark overcoat. "He ditched this when I chased him earlier. I think he was trying to blend in better with the crowd."

"Whoa, row back your boat. Catch me up a little bit."

HONK! BLARE! WAIL! HONK! BLARE! WAIL!

Grayson blew out a breath and shook his head but motioned for her to continue.

"Who ditched this?" He looked at the coat.

"Your suspect. At least, I think he is your suspect."

Grayson narrowed his eyes, intent on catching every word she spoke.

"An older man's been following me all day. I've caught him lurking, pretending to be engrossed in products in nearby booths—once he was even reading an upside-down box of cards—but, I don't know," she shrugged, "something about him felt weird, and not necessarily in a bad way. While Violet and I were talking to Olivia, I spotted him watching me from behind the tent flaps on Eli's booth. I was curious, so I decided to talk to him but the moment he saw me walking his way, he bolted."

Grayson raked a hand through his hair—his heart suddenly pounding in his chest. He closed his eyes and took a deep breath.

"And you decided it would be a good idea to follow him?" he asked incredulously.

She nodded. "Ran to catch up with him, actually," she said, one eye half shut, and her face contorted in apprehension, anticipating his less-than-happy response.

"Everly, sweetheart, darling, love of my life, why on earth would you do that?"

She sobered quickly. "Did you just call me the love of your life?" she asked, a grin starting at the corners of her mouth.

"Come on, Albuquerque, you're missing the point. How can I keep you safe if you're going to run off half-cocked after some stranger who may have already put one man in the hospital?"

HONK! BLARE! WAIL! HONK! BLARE! WAIL!

Grayson picked up his radio. "Could someone please shut off that alarm? I'm on my way!"

She held out the coat for him again. "I'm fine. He ran. There were a lot of people around. I can't imagine I was in any real danger."

"And if he'd led you into an empty alleyway, would you have followed?"

It took her a moment to respond.

"Grayson, sweetheart, darling, love of my life, I am *all right*. Go!"

HONK! BLARE! WAIL! Beep. Beep. Nothing.

Finally!

He eyed her for a moment, glancing her over as if to verify she was indeed all right. He had just found her. His reason. His match. His person. The mere idea of losing her now set his nerves on edge.

"Go!" She pointed.

With an exasperated tilt of his head, he grabbed the coat and headed back into the blissfully unaware crowd. By the time he reached his truck, there was no sign of the man.

"Who has the visual?" Grayson asked, searching the faces of his deputies.

"As soon as the alarm sounded, he took off," Deputy Gonzalez said. "We tried to follow on foot, but we lost him behind Santa's Village." The man was still working to catch his breath after the chase.

"Did anyone get a good look at him?" Grayson asked while patting down the coat Everly had found and reaching into its pockets.

"He's older," one officer stated. "White hair or gray maybe."

"But not so old that he's out of shape because he was fast," another said.

Several grunts of agreement followed.

"What you got there, boss?" Deputy Gonzalez asked.

Grayson discovered a small phone in the coat's pocket and when he pulled it out, a new message appeared on the screen from an apparently unrecognized phone number.

"If you don't want anyone else to get hurt, go to the confectionery and purchase a single small, red organza bag. Place the flash drive inside, then tape it to the underside of Santa's sleigh," he read the message aloud.

Organza bag? What bad guy talks like that?

Grayson had so many questions. Had the man who'd been following Everly left the phone in his pocket on purpose as a way to contact them? If so, was Everly the intended recipient of this message? Had he known that she would turn it over to law enforcement? If so, had the message been intended for him? And if it was the drive he was looking for, why would he believe that she would have brought it here with her?

His mind raced with dozens of scenarios, possibilities, and more questions. There had to be more to the picture than what they were seeing. Something vital was missing, but what?

"It's likely a burner," Grayson concluded, handing the phone to a nearby officer, who opened an evidence bag so he could drop it inside. "Take Wilson and see what you can find—fingerprints, contacts, history, anything."

The officer nodded and responded, "Yes, sir."

"Gonzalez, you're with me. The rest of you will be positioned strategically around the festival with two of you stationed near the confectionery, two by Santa's sleigh and reindeer corral and the rest, let's ditch the security jackets for plain clothes coats over your vests and blend in with the crowd, keeping your eyes and ears open. We have no idea what this guy is planning, and our ultimate goal is to catch this guy, and making sure everyone stays safe out there. Report any suspicious behavior or individuals, and stay in pairs. Keep your radios on."

"Yes, sir," several officers responded at once as they left to their assignments.

Now, let's see what you're trying so hard to get.

He retrieved his laptop from the truck.

"Where are we on the clinic?" he asked Marcus while he booted the computer.

"They've only had two stitches cases all week…" he pulled a notebook from his pocket. "…a seven-year-old kid with a laceration to his forehead and a thirty-seven-year-old male who shot himself in the foot with a nail gun."

"So, nothing."

"No, sir."

Everly's thumb drive was still safely tucked into the coin pocket of his jeans, but he'd already taken the initiative to download the contents onto his computer this morning, so it wouldn't take long to load. As he scanned the contents, he shook his head in disbelief.

There, laid out on the drive, were the personal files of one Mr. Peter Jacobi. Apparently, Everly's new boss was deeply involved in several counts of criminal activity and had documented what appeared to be each and every illegal transaction he'd made over the last ten years—including names, headshots, blackmail information, and more on each of his associates. It even contained the address of his 'fixer' as he called him in the records. No wonder Mr. Jacobi wanted this drive back so badly. It would put him and his cohorts away for a very long time.

Everly must have mixed up the two drives and taken Jacobi's by mistake.

"Do we want to set up a decoy?" Marcus asked.

Grayson thought for a moment. "Does it seem like an odd request to you?" he asked, musing. "He would have had no way of knowing whether or not she would even have it with her. And why would she carry it around with her? To a Christmas festival of all places. Unless, he had…"

"Contacted her before the festival?" Gonzalez provided.

Everly hadn't made any mention of having received any peculiar or threatening messages.

"Yes, why would he wait to contact her at the festival. It

just doesn't make sense."

"It definitely doesn't feel like the work of a professional."

"That's what I thought too." As he quickly continued to glance over the files, he noted that one folder contained the names and activities of several people in very high places—judges, police chiefs, politicians, and attorneys, businessmen, and more. There were even candid surveillance-type photos in almost every file. It would be reckless to upload everything directly onto the servers as they could easily be deleted by the right people and even more lives would be put in danger.

"We could set something up to try to drive out whoever sent that text. But something is telling me it's not our fixer. However, if he's the one who has been following Everly, he will hopefully be able to provide us with some answers."

Grayson uploaded the criminal activity files into the system and prepared to make the necessary phone calls. He guessed there would be several arrests by morning. Including Mr. Peter Jacobi. As he went to click on the file of the fixer, the name on a different folder jumped out at him.

Jason Quinn, BHPD – Deceased.

What were the odds that wasn't Everly's father? He made a mental note to look over the file later. Right now, they had a suspect to apprehend.

He opened the folder containing information on the fixer and opened the photo with the cleanest shot of the man's face. He increased the size of it on his laptop and turned it around to show Gonzalez.

"That's him all right," Marcus confirmed. "The man who we chased behind Santa's Village."

Grayson clicked on his radio.

"We are looking for a Mr.," he looked closer at the screen, "Ward Hughes. Fifty-eight. Six feet tall, brown eyes, approximately one hundred ninety pounds."

The file placed the man's address in Randolph, New Mexico, and even went so far as to say that he lived with his eighty-seven-year-old mother and a cat named Fred. It was all too neat. Surely, no one could be so stupid as to keep records like this sitting out unprotected on a desk in plain sight in an office building.

Unless Jacobi had been the one to mix up the drives.

"Okay, get this picture out to every officer on site," he told his deputy. "I have some questions. But let's bring him in quietly. I'd rather not disrupt the festival. I would never hear the end of it from my mother."

With the information safely uploaded, the drive no longer bore any intrinsic value. But Grayson couldn't shake the feeling that Hughes was smarter than his boss. He shook his head. This was the kind of information that got people killed. With all the data they'd uncovered, there would likely be no deals to be made, and it was possible Jacobi had sent more than one person to try to retrieve it.

"Let's get a decoy in place," Grayson said with a nod. "Feel like buying some chocolate?"

"I'll do it," Wes joined them, his breathing a little ragged. "Decoy. Chocolate. Sounds like me."

"Nice of you to join us, Deputy."

"I'll have you know, your booth is safely back in your mother's hands."

"Thanks for stepping in. And you're just in time."

Grayson took a few minutes to fill Wes in on everything that had occurred, and while they bounced some other ideas and theories off one another, they determined that attempting to draw out the suspect and getting him away from the festival would be the best course of action. So, Wes was given a small pebble about the size of a thumb drive to use as a decoy in the bag.

If Hughes was expecting Everly, he'd be sorely disappointed.

A quick phone call would assure that she would stay as far away from the confectionery as possible.

No answer.

"Come on, sweetheart," he mumbled under his breath.

He tried again.

Still no answer.

I'm sure she's fine, he told himself. She wasn't alone. When he'd left her, she'd been with his family, and he had to trust that they would watch out for her.

"Let's roll."

Grayson watched the crowd, the hairs on the back of his neck standing on end. He knew Hughes couldn't be working alone. While the thought had crossed his mind several times over the last half an hour he still couldn't fit the pieces together. He'd thought about bringing his laptop and using it as cover, continuing to search the files, but he didn't want to risk alerting Hughes that the information had been compromised—though, the man had to know they would have downloaded the files.

So, what is there to gain now by obtaining the worthless shell of evidence?

Eli Thomas sat on a chair right outside of the little library façade on the set that had been created as scenery for Santa's Village. A large group had gathered around him while he read from what Grayson guessed was his new Christmas children's book based on stories from Silver Falls.

Rachel stood at the front of the audience, just off to the side, beaming up at him. Whether she wanted to admit it or not, she was smitten with the writer. Anyone with eyes could see it. One officer stood only a few feet from her watching the crowd, and another stood behind the stage, overlooking the author and the group from a different vantage point.

A quick scan of the area showed the plain clothes officers standing in line, walking the streets, and he noted the two officers patrolling the area around the confectionery.

Good.

It didn't take long for Hughes to appear. Now adorned in

a dark brown jacket with a cotton hood, he slowly approached the confectionery where Wes still stood in line, stopping to peruse several of the booths as he closed in. But it was odd. Hughes had not looked at Wes or the confectionery line even once.

Grayson watched intently as the officers communicated through seemingly random gestures—a tip of a hat, rubbing a nose, blowing a gum bubble—all signals keeping him apprised of what was happening from every angle.

Hughes didn't seem to be in a big rush, he just strolled along booth after booth, casually browsing the festival's offerings and occasionally glancing up toward the food booths. Wes reached up to scratch the back of his head, indicating he'd seen their target and was prepared to do what was necessary.

As Grayson prepared to close in, he followed Hughes' gaze and caught a glimpse of Everly and several members of his family, and hers, making their way toward the food booths.

Not now. Why couldn't she have just answered her phone?

More questions bombarded his mind at the sight of her.

Why had Hughes let Everly see him earlier? Any fixer worth his salt wouldn't be seen unless he'd wanted to be. Why not just break into the house while they were all at the festival when there was no one there to stop him from looking for what he wanted? He had to know she was staying in the barn.

No, Hughes wanted something more, but Grayson's gut told him that the old man was a pawn in a much bigger game. He stood in place, pivoting in a circle, scanning the bustling crowd, looking for anything else that might indicate the fixer was working with someone else, but everything seemed to be in its place. Still, he'd not sent as much as a fleeting glance at the confectionery line.

Then it dawned on him.

Everly.

It was the only thing that made any sense. They not only wanted the drive, they wanted her. If they suspected for even a moment that she had looked inside those files, that she knew what they contained, she would have a huge target on her back. And now, so would he.

He immediately scanned the rooftops. If Jacobi was as connected as those files made it seem, something very bad was about to go down in his town unless he could figure out the piece they were missing and put a stop to it. There was no evidence of a sniper, but that was not uncommon. They were paid to be invisible.

There was no indication that anyone was watching the confectionery line. The decoy was not working. So, the only option was to get Hughes off the street and get some answers. Then, he needed to get to Everly.

"Moving in," he called on his radio.

Grayson casually strode across the square and walked right up behind the man.

"It's over, Mr. Hughes," he said quietly. "Don't make a scene." Grayson's hand sat on the Glock at his hip and had the other on the man's shoulder.

Hughes turned around, and in an attempt to body-check Grayson, who had been prepared and stood his ground, ended up on his backside. He pulled himself to his feet, but rather than try to go through the sheriff again, he darted in one direction, then another, and was stopped at each side by an officer in waiting.

"You need to come with us," Grayson said sternly in low tones as not to alert the entire courtyard. He rotated the man as discreetly as possible, turning him away from the row of food booths he'd been watching earlier, and placed cuffs on his wrists.

"You need to listen to me very carefully," Hughes said quietly. "They could be watching."

"Who could be watching?" Grayson normally may have rejected such a conspiracy-like comment, but his gut had felt heavy since they'd arrived in Town Square. If he was going to do his job well and keep the people he loved safe, he couldn't dismiss anything right now, no matter how ludicrous it might sound.

"I don't know who he sent, but it's Peter Jacobi pulling the strings. You don't understand, I need to protect Everly Quinn. You need to let me go."

"Not likely." He glanced over his shoulder at his family, now stopped at the German food booth, but neither Everly nor Violet were among them.

His heart skipped a beat.

Where did she go? He scanned the area immediately around the food booth, but neither sister was anywhere to be seen. *Maybe they've gone to the restroom*, he reasoned.

"Were you protecting Everly when you hit Frank Collins over the head?"

"I'm telling you, it wasn't me. I know what it looks like, believe me."

Grayson grabbed the man's arm and walked with him behind the confectionery to a little alcove on the far side of the corner gazebo, followed by several officers.

"That's easy enough to confirm. The suspect would have cut himself pretty badly at the mechanic shop—enough to leave a trail of blood evidence behind." Grayson wished he could put a rush on those samples he'd collected and have results in a few hours like they did in the movies, but alas, he'd still have to wait the typical two weeks—maybe twelve days if they pushed it—for the forensics lab in Denver to process it.

"No wounds," Hughes said, pulling up his sleeves and pant pockets.

After a quick frisk job, pulling a solitary knife from the man's boot, Grayson was satisfied that Hughes did not bear any wounds that would have left the amount of blood the suspect had left behind from the glass embedded in the door at the garage.

"We're wasting time, Sheriff. Everly is in danger," Hughes

persisted.

"What do you know about Everly Quinn?" he asked.

"I know that you care for her. I know she feels the same."

"How could you know that?" He looked over his shoulder. Still no sign of Everly and a pit now weighed heavy in his gut.

"Look, I've done a lot of things in my past I'm not proud of, and I did my time, but that's not me anymore."

"Where is she, Hughes?" His heart thumped loudly, the whooshing reaching his ears.

"She was about to order food from one of the food booths just before you cuffed me," he said, exasperated. "The longer it takes you to believe me..."

"That's the problem, old man, I do believe you. And she's not there anymore."

"What do you mean?" Hughes whipped around to look for Everly by the German booth. "Violet's gone too."

"Marcus," Grayson called to Deputy Gonzalez, "will you escort Mr. Hughes over to the jail?" He motioned at the building across the street next to the old library. The Silver Falls Town Square still boasted several of the original structures that had been built over a hundred and fifty years ago. A jailhouse was among them and, while the buildings were often used as tourist destinations for the rustic part of town, the jail cells were still functioning, and they'd seen fit on occasion to use them. He tossed his deputy the set of old sheriff's keys.

"Yes, sir."

"Listen, Sheriff, you need to let me go," Hughes called after him. "You don't know what you're up against."

Grayson grabbed Wes, who had jumped out of the confectionery line to join them in the arrest.

"What is it, Gray?" he asked.

"You need me, Kane," Hughes called out, a desperate edge to his voice. "Don't walk away, please. Grayson!" he finally yelled his name.

Every logical bone in his body screamed that he would be following protocol to have Ward Hughes arrested on suspicion of attempted murder, but he stopped, turned around, and marched back to face him.

"You tell me right now who you are to Everly and why I should let you go."

"That little girl wouldn't know me from Adam, but I know her." Hughes' eyes were like steel as they met Grayson's.

"Explain."

"There's no time."

"Explain!"

"I was a fixer for a lot of years for a lot of bad people. I was arrested the night that Everly was born. By Jason Quinn, her father."

"You're not making a very good case for yourself," Grayson turned to walk away.

"He changed the course of my life that day, Sheriff. It took time, but we became close friends. A part of me died the night he was killed, and I swore that I would watch out for the girls in secret so as to not bring any of my past anywhere near them. I cannot let anything happen to her. You have to let me go. I can help!"

"Sheriff?" Marcus asked as if wanting to know how to proceed.

"I trust that gut of yours more than you know," Wes said over his shoulder, "but you need to really consider the possible implications of what you're considering."

His cousin was right. Grayson knew even entertaining the idea was absurd, but if there was any truth to what Hughes said, he could be helpful. He fixed his eyes on the man's and searched them for any hint of deception. He could count on one hand the number of times he'd been wrong about a person after looking them in the eye.

"If anything happens to her..." Grayson's jaw flexed. He

couldn't finish his threat.

"And I would deserve it for the past things I've done."

"Let him go," he whispered, his eyes still set on Hughes.

"Sheriff?" Marcus questioned.

Grayson looked up at his deputy and nodded.

Once he was out of the cuffs, Hughes held out his hand expectantly.

"My knife."

With one more exasperated breath, Grayson handed the weapon back to the man.

"Spread out. Everyone be on the lookout for Everly Quinn." Then, he realized that none of them knew her. His heart had recognized her as if they'd known one another a lifetime, but by every other standard, it had only been days.

My phone.

He pulled the device from his pocket and pulled up the selfie they had taken before the Guardian Run. "This," he showed it to the others, "is Everly." He quickly sent a copy to Marcus. "Get this image on all of their phones. I want her found."

"Yes, Boss."

"Don't make me regret this," he told Hughes. "Come on."

Grayson and Hughes ran together toward the food court with Wes right behind them.

It only took a moment before they reached Holden, Landon, and Owen who were still waiting for their food.

"I wonder if Rachel knows that man is engaged," Landon was saying as they arrived, glancing over to Santa's Village where Eli Thomas had just finished his reading.

Grayson followed his gaze to see Rachel laughing as she helped Eli with the microphone on his lapel.

"They were friends in college," Grayson said dismissively. "Have you seen Everly?"

"Yes, friends." Landon nodded, disbelief written all over his face.

"The man is braver than I," Holden said with a nod at Santa's Village. "If Olivia saw me flirting with an *old friend from college* like that, well, I'd probably end up on the wrong side of the dirt in one of her novels."

Owen and Landon laughed, but Grayson didn't have time to engage in their playful banter.

"Where is she?" he asked again in a rush.

"Olivia?" Holden pointed back toward the little author's booth area.

"Gray, what's wrong?" Landon asked, concern now etched on his brow as he took a step toward him. "Where's who?"

"Everly. Where is she? I just saw her over here with you a few minutes ago."

"She's just right over there…" Everly's brother-in-law's voice trailed as he pointed toward the food court entrance with two giant candy canes topped by a sign labeled Candy Cane Grove. "That's weird, she was just talking with her ex's fiancée over there a minute ago."

"You must be Owen," Grayson said, extending his hand. "Her ex has a fiancée?"

"I think she called her Sheila. My wife would know."

"Where is your wife?"

"Present." Everly's little sister trudged up the slight incline with a finger raised in the air. "I do not recommend drinking more than one Santa-sized beverage when you are nine months pregnant," she said, returning to the group from the bathrooms. "But it's nearly impossible to resist something that tastes like Christmas in a cup." She took her still half-full drink from her husband with a smile and took a sip.

"Violet," Grayson said, his plea growing more urgent, "was your sister with you?" He looked behind the pregnant woman but didn't see her. "Where is Everly?" He hated sounding like a broken record.

"She stopped to help that backstabbing publicist fiancée

of Eli's pick up some packages and boxes when she slipped on the ice and fell in her silly high-heeled boots. How my sister can even look at that woman is beyond me."

Grayson remembered Olivia had told him about the woman who had convinced Eli to call off their wedding.

"So, that idiot is engaged to the same publicist who said Everly was bad for his image?"

"That's the one. Sheila Reed." By the way Violet was squeezing her cup, it was a good thing that it was of the hard variety and not one of those little disposable plastic kinds. "I know," her demeanor suddenly lightened. "We should actually be grateful to her, though, or Everly would have never found you."

Hughes hit Grayson on the arm. "If Sheila Reed is Shane Reed's granddaughter, we have a problem. Shane Reed and Peter Jacobi's father, Raymond, are the co-founders of R&J Media—"

"Where Everly worked—"

"Until recently," Hughes finished with a nod.

"Peter just took over the operations of the company, but he's a bad seed, nothing like his father. If Sheila is involved with him in any way—"

"Then Everly could be…" Grayson swallowed. He couldn't think that way. Wouldn't. They had to find her and fast.

"Violet, where did you last see your sister?"

"Slow down, little brother," Holden said, placing a hand on his shoulder. "What's wrong?" His eyes flitted between Grayson and Hughes.

"It's Everly. She's in danger. Help me find her."

CHAPTER FIFTEEN

"I wanted to apologize about earlier," Sheila said as they passed one of the little ornament booths. "I don't know what gets into me sometimes. And I should have listened to you about the boots." She smiled sheepishly.

While the event committee, or rather, the Kane men and some of their relations, had done a great job of shoveling the main walkways of the festival route, there were still many patches of ice that appeared to be resisting the melting-salt that had been sprinkled over the cobblestone paths.

Sheila's fashionable heeled boots were no match for this weather. Everly laughed to herself thinking of how far she'd come in just a few days, embarrassed to think about the heeled strappy sandals she'd been wearing on the first night. She looked down, grateful for the heavy-traction, insulated boots the girls had lent to her.

Just on their short trek to the backstage area behind the false fronts of Santa's Village, Sheila had nearly fallen several times and had clung to Everly's arm for support—while Everly had carried the new box of Eli's books.

By the time they'd reached the stage, Eli had already

finished his reading and had been surrounded by dozens of young adoring fans, so his publicist had picked up a box cutter and proceeded to cut through the cardboard to take out several books and walk them out, without so much as a wobble, to the cashier.

No way. Everly glanced out through one of the false doors and saw that they had brought in some real reindeer, and they were now corralled with full harnesses next to the stage and Santa's sleigh. The caretakers were passing out something that patrons were feeding to the animals.

Could this town seriously be any more magical for Christmas?

She looked down at her watch. By the time she got back to the others, her schnitzel would be cold, but she could get Violet and they could go feed the reindeer. She quickly made her way to the far end of Santa's Village, but not before Sheila walked back through the stage door.

"Everly," she called out.

Almost.

She slowly pivoted on one foot to face the woman.

"I have actually been meaning to talk to you." Her voice was tinged with what appeared to be genuine humility. "Can I buy you a coffee?"

"I'm good. Thank you though. I really should be getting back."

"I'd really like to talk to you if you can spare a moment."

"What could you possibly say, Sheila?" Everly had thought about what she would say to the woman a thousand times over, but none of that seemed important now.

"That I know I made a mistake when I gave Eli the advice to break up with you—that marrying you would ruin his career." She took a ginger step toward her. "It truly wasn't about you as much as it had been about promoting him." Her forehead was crinkled with concern. "It was my job..." She raised her hands in front of her in a shrug, and for the first time, Everly noted a dark, wet patch on Sheila's sleeve and what looked like blood on the side of her wrist trailing up her arm.

"...and men like Eli tend to become more successful when they are single," Sheila continued to talk as if she hadn't noticed anything out of the ordinary. "Or at least when they appear to be single." She took another step forward. "I didn't stop long enough to consider what it would do to you. I'm sorry."

While that was the last thing Everly had expected to come out of Sheila's mouth—she had been prepared for snark and disdain, not apologetic and cordial after all—and it was a little disarming, she couldn't stop staring at the woman's arm.

"Sheila are you all right?" Everly asked, rushing toward the woman, her eyes focused on her arm. "Did you do that when you fell? Why didn't you tell me? We need to get you over to the first aid booth. Here," she reached out, "let me see."

The woman twisted her arm up to look at it. "Oh, it's bleeding again?" She shook her head. "I got a flat tire on my first night here and would you believe they do not have Triple A? The jack slipped because of the snowy road, and it sliced up my arm pretty good. The doc gave me some bandages, but I left them in my truck. Would you care to accompany me?"

Everly really wanted to get back to her family, but couldn't bring herself to leave a bleeding woman. No matter who that woman might be.

Blood.

She shook her head. Grayson had told her that whoever had broken into the garage and hit that poor mechanic over the head had cut themselves badly.

Impossible.

"Are you sure you wouldn't rather head down to the first aid booth? I'm pretty sure they have a doctor on-site." She pointed across the street to the only booth on the corner of the big church that sat there with a white flag bearing a red cross hung from the roof.

"I'd rather not make such a fuss. It's just a little scratch."

By the amount of blood on her arm, Everly guessed it was no scratch, but she relented.

"Where are you parked?"

"In the back, just down the path past that food court…Candy Cane something or other."

Odd.

Sheila walked over and linked her good arm through hers.

The situation had become a little unsettling and Everly scanned the distant crowd for any sign of Grayson, her sister, or anyone familiar. There was no one over by the German food booth, and the farther they got away from the crowd, the more uneasy Everly felt.

"Maybe you should keep that elevated," she said, trying not to get lost in her own thoughts.

How did I get hustled into this? she wondered. *Helping her ex-fiancé's fiancée. Who'd have thought?*

She'd done her good deed by helping her out today, so why was she still stuck arm-in-arm with the woman who'd single-handedly ruined the last year of her life?

"You know, I should have realized that the people here would be so supportive of his writing, and that friend of his from college…" she paused.

"Rachel?"

"Yes. Rachel…McClarin has done a really good job of advertising the book here in Silver Falls." The heel on Sheila's boot broke off and she nearly fell again, tugging Everly's arm downward.

Seriously?

She picked up the broken piece of her boot and trudged on with a lopsided gait up the remaining frosted path.

"I think she likes him, *my* fiancé." Sheila's grip on her arm had grown a little too tight. "The way she is always smiling at him, and touching him, and always doing things for him." The smile on her face appeared just a bit too rehearsed. "She's pretty. Don't you think she's pretty?" She tilted her head toward Everly but did not look at her.

"I do think Rachel is pretty," she responded.

The east parking lot was filled with empty vehicles. Not another soul in sight. Everly's nerves were on edge, panic rising in her chest.

"But he's *your* fiancé, Sheila," she managed to say. "You win."

The festive music and joyful chatter of the festival now seemed a little too distant for her comfort.

They approached a large, dark green truck with an extended cab. Sheila reached into her pant pockets and all the lights on the vehicle flashed briefly, and she stepped in front of Everly and opened the back cab door.

"I was sorry to hear that you had lost your job. I always thought you were one of the best."

"How would you know that, Sheila?"

"I understand that you didn't want anyone else to be able to have your designs either, so you took your portfolio with you."

Everly took a step backward.

"There is no way you could know that…"

The flash drive.

The blood.

The impossible was quickly turning to reality.

"Have you had a chance to review your *portfolio* since you left? Of course, you haven't. Why would you? It's not like you'd need it in a place like this."

Everly turned to run. She needed to get away from this crazy woman.

Click.

"I wouldn't."

She froze. She closed her eyes.

A gun?

Her heart nearly jumped from her chest, and she had to

fight to keep her breathing in check. She'd fallen right into whatever sick game Sheila was playing, and it wasn't looking good for her.

Slowly, she turned back to face the woman.

"I don't want Eli anymore, Sheila. Like I said before, you won."

"You think I won?" She laughed a maniacal, twisted sort of laugh that contorted her features into something unrecognizable. "Eli is weak. He's a children's book author, a LARPer for heaven's sake, an 'I enjoy long walks on the beach' kinda guy. Ack. Handsome, I'll give him that, but beta male is not really my style."

"Sheila, I think you've lost too much blood and I'm worried that cut might be infected. You're not making any sense." Everly braved a step toward her. "If we can just get you in to see a doctor, I'm sure they'll get you all fixed up as good as new."

"Don't patronize me, *Miss Quinn*. I know the power that comes with this little machine. I know you'd say anything to get me to put it down. But what you don't know is that we're going to go for a little ride, and you're going to take me to that flash drive that you took off Jacobi's desk."

"What is so special about a creative director's media portfolio?"

"Are you really that dumb or do you just play it well? You took Peter's drive by mistake, and the information on that drive is way more valuable than you could ever be."

"And if I refuse to come with you?"

An odd, victorious smile touched her lips. "I'll kill him." She shifted the gun to face a wide-eyed Eli.

Where had he come from and how had he known to come here?

"Sheila?" Eli's expression was a mixture of hurt, anger, and shock.

Everly's heartbeat quickened, and she rushed to explain. "I

don't have the drive anymore, Sheila. I gave it to Grayson."

The woman's jaw clenched, her free hand balled into a fist.

"Then, you, Miss Everly Quinn, are the only leverage I need."

CRACK!

The distinct sound of a gunshot rang in Grayson's trained ears, slicing through the music and laughter of happy festivalgoers. The sharp crack pierced the frigid air and sent birds scattering from nearby trees, but between the games and other activities, the crowd hadn't seemed to notice.

"That came from behind the library and town offices," he yelled out to Wes and Hughes who were both within hearing range.

Without hesitation, Grayson sprinted up the pathway between Candy Cane Grove and Santa's Village, his heart pounding wildly in his chest as he ripped his radio from his belt.

"I need an assist. All officers converge on the east parking lot." Thoughts of Everly raced through his mind and he prepared himself for what he might find.

Surprisingly, Hughes kept pace with the younger men, and it offered him some odd level of comfort to know the man had experience. As they reached the edge of the last building, they gathered at the corner with Grayson in the front.

He darted a look around the brick and his heart flipped in gratitude at the sight of Everly still standing and unhurt. A look of horror maligned her beautiful face as she looked over at the ground next to her.

Eli Thomas lay lifeless on the ground, and Sheila stood in front of them both, her gun still aimed toward her fiancé.

He dropped his head, then looked over at Wes and

motioned for him to section off the path so that no one could get through. The last thing he needed was for civilians to get caught in any crossfire.

The deputy nodded his understanding and headed back down the trail.

Hughes left his side, running quietly back down the trail until he would be out of Sheila's view, then crossed the street, using the trees that had been set up for Candy Cane Grove as cover.

Good thinking.

"You just lost your only piece of leverage on me," Everly called out. "I'll never go with you now."

"You think you can run from me? Your precious sheriff has something I want, something that is worth a lot. And if you don't do exactly as I say—"

"What? You're going to kill me too? Then where will you be? Grayson is smart. It won't take him long to figure out what's going on and you'll never get what you're looking for. So, what's the play here, Sheila?" There was a catch in her voice. She was crying. "You'll never be able to go home. Not after this. Not after...Eli."

That's it, sweetheart, keep her talking.

He just needed enough time for Marcus and the others to get in place.

"Oh, Everly," Sheila said, her gun wavering as she spoke, "you really have no idea what you are talking about. Once I've secured that drive, it will be like I have a get-out-of-jail-free card. All of this," she looked around as if 'this' was something tangible, "will go away. I'll be spending my days on the most beautiful beaches in the world. I'll have enough money to buy my way into a new home, a new life without all the corporate drivel."

"You know you'll have to kill me,..."

Okay, sweetheart, maybe stop talking now.

"...and then you'll have to kill the sheriff."

"It's a small price to pay. Now," Sheila's focus became laser-like as she stared at Everly, "slowly walk toward me. We're going to get out that phone you've been dying to use and call that handsome sheriff of yours."

Grayson fumbled to retrieve his phone from his pocket. He didn't need his ringtone to give away his position. Once silenced, he pulled the Glock from his holster and waited.

"He probably already knows what's—"

"Stop wasting my time!" Sheila yelled. "Get over here."

Everly complied, pulling her phone from her pocket.

"Now, get in."

Sheila stepped forward just enough to shut the back cab door and open the front.

"You heard me, get in." She clicked a button on her fob and the truck roared to life.

A glint of light caught Grayson's eye.

Granddad? How had he known?

Ian Redbourne had climbed, unnoticed, into the back of a pickup a couple of rows behind Sheila's. His rifle in hand, he leaned over the cab, using the roof as a support, and had it aimed at the woman who had orchestrated so much of Everly's recent turmoil, though he'd only have a partial view from his vantage point until she headed around to the driver's seat of the truck.

He glanced up, and both men exchanged nods.

"Come on, Marcus," he whispered under his breath.

Finally, he noticed a flicker of movement from the corner of his eye. Deputy Gonzalez appeared at the opposite end of the parking lot and, keeping low, was making his way toward them. It was time. He caught his deputy's eye, and with a few gestures, told him to stay alert and be ready.

As Everly moved to step up onto the runners of the truck, she shoulder-checked Sheila hard into the door and the gun went off.

Grayson's world exploded inside him, and he clung to the

split-second prayer he offered.

"Now!" he screamed, adrenaline coursing through his veins, his heart hammering in his chest as the air around him seemed to fall silent in the midst of his charge. His mouth went dry, but everything came into focus, seeming to move in slowed motion until he reached his intended target.

"Sheila Reed," he yelled, now just feet away from her, "you are surrounded. There's no way out."

The sound of several cocking guns was like music to his ears.

An eerie giggle turned into a delirious laugh. The irrational woman had gained the upper hand on Everly, who now turned to face him, blood oozing down the front of her shirt and Sheila's hand at her throat.

"I'm sorry," Everly mouthed the words, her tearstained cheeks flushed with color.

"Sheriff Kane, it's nice to finally meet you in person," Sheila said as if they were meeting under any normal circumstances.

"I'm afraid I can't say the same," he said, his gun still trained on the woman.

"Miss Quinn has informed me that the little trinket I'm looking for is now in your possession. I'm going to need you to hand it over." Her eyes held a manic glint.

He knew all too well that a desperate woman would do desperate things, and with Everly in the balance, he decided to play into her delusions. He took his finger off the trigger of his gun and held it up, broadside against his palm.

"I have it right here." He slipped his fingers into the small coin pocket of his jeans and pulled it out, holding it up to show her.

Everly's brows scrunched as she met his eyes.

"Let her go," he said, not taking his eyes off of Everly.

"Toss it into the truck," she said, the tension palpable.

The moment he flung the drive into the air, Sheila's gaze

was diverted as she watched its trajectory. Everly reached up, seizing the woman's forearm in a vicelike grip.

Sheila screamed out in intense agony, and Everly shot forward, but her captor reached out and caught her by the hair, pulling her back toward her. Cradling her wounded arm close to her body, she stepped up onto the runner, heaving Everly along with her.

Grayson charged forward. Sheila's gun fired again, but the shot went wide. Unwilling to be deterred, he returned his grip to his gun, closed the distance between them with a single lunge, and raised his weapon steadily mere inches from her face.

"Let. Her. Go," he said more calmly than he felt. He reached out, pried the gun from her hand, and scooped Everly out of the truck and into his arms.

Keenly aware of the movement around him, Grayson finally breathed a relieved sigh when Hughes opened the driver's side door and dragged Sheila to the ground.

Deputy Gonzalez called on his radio. "We're going to need a medic in the east parking lot."

Grayson buried his face in Everly's hair, then shot backward, scanning her body for the source of the blood he'd seen trailing down the front of her.

"It's not mine," she said, shaking her head.

Relief washed over him as he delved his arms fully around her, lifting her off the ground, and squeezing her close.

"I thought I'd lost you."

"Grayson, sweetheart, love of my life," Everly gasped with some difficulty, "I can't breathe."

A loud guffaw escaped him as he relaxed his grip and set her back on the ground, but he didn't let go. He never wanted to let go. He bent his forehead to rest against hers.

"You could never lose me, Grayson Kane," Everly said. "You found me." She nudged his face upward until their eyes met. "I am home."

He claimed her lips in his.

"I guess it's a good thing for all of us that Sheila is a horrible shot."

Everly broke their kiss, her head shot in the direction of her ex. Eli stood up and brushed debris from his pants. She jumped out of his arms and ran toward the man, gracing him with a hug and a delighted squeal.

Realization dawned on Grayson that Eli had been playing dead for the better part of a quarter-hour, and an added measure of relief overshadowed any hint of jealousy he might be feeling. He chuckled, then strode over to where the two stood and enveloped them both in a bear hug.

"Eli?" Rachel's shaky voice brought Grayson's head up.

She was accompanied by one of the other officers.

"I found her hiding right over there in the stairwell of the town offices, Sheriff," he said. "I think she might be in shock. Says she saw everything."

"Thanks, Wilson. I've got her from here." He stepped back away from Everly and Eli and held open his arm, inviting her in.

Rachel slipped her arm around him, resting her head on his chest. But it wasn't him she was there to see.

Grayson cleared his throat.

Eli and Everly looked up and then men exchanged girls. Rachel ran to Eli, her hand sweetly on his face, then without warning, she kissed him hard. After a moment of perceived shock, Eli relaxed, deepening their kiss and pulling her into his embrace.

Grayson laughed again.

"As Shakespeare would say, 'All's well that ends well.'"

CHAPTER SIXTEEN

"I still can't believe Sheila is the one who ran me off the road." Everly sat on the couch with her legs tucked up beneath her, sipping her morning cocoa in her Christmas movie pajamas with Olivia, Penelope, and Violet who had come over first thing this morning.

"I guess in that way, we should be thanking her," Penelope said from her position on the floor in front of the couch. "Because if she hadn't done that, we would have never met." She leaned back, pressing into Everly's knee but didn't take her eyes from the photos she was scanning through on her camera. "I'm just so glad that Frank is going to be all right."

"Me too." She couldn't help but feel guilty for what had happened to that poor mechanic.

"It wasn't your fault," Violet reminded her—always seeming to know what she was thinking.

Everly reached over and squeezed her sister's hand.

Grayson had spent the better half of the evening last night talking to Sheila and had to be back in the office this morning to finish up his paperwork, but he hoped, with any luck, that the U.S. Marshals would be there to pick Sheila up to transfer down to Albuquerque in time for them to make it to the tree-lighting tonight.

"To hear Grayson tell it, eleven arrest warrants already went out this morning." Olivia came in from the kitchen with two plates in her hand. "Okay, our charming little brother got up before Brewster this morning to come out to the barn and use the kitchen here to make his famous breakfast casserole because he'd wanted to make sure 'Albuquerque' had something good to eat for breakfast."

"Awwwww…" all three women sighed in unison, and Everly felt the heat rise happily in her cheeks.

Everly giggled. "Who's Brewster?"

Penelope and Olivia both laughed. "The rooster."

Olivia handed her the first plate with a large square piece and Violet the second before heading back into the kitchen for hers and Penelope's.

It was so good to have her sister with her on Christmas Eve. It had been a long time since they'd spent the holiday together.

When Violet and Owen had arrived this morning, he had been excited for the opportunity to help the others with some of the chores around the ranch and so, for the moment, it was just the women. This closeness with other women was something Everly had never had before—other than with Violet, but even then, it was hard to come by since they lived so far apart.

The food smelled so good, but she was a little wary of it. She'd never heard of breakfast casserole before and wondered if mixing breakfast foods together was actually a good idea. She picked up her fork and cautiously took a bite.

Delicious. She closed her eyes and relished the warm taste of it.

"Good right?"

Knock. Knock.

"Are you expecting anyone?" Pen asked Olivia as she returned with plates for each of them.

"Yes, but he's early, Holden and Ian aren't back yet." She set her food down onto the coffee table, then ran into the office to answer the door.

Since the blinds were raised on the glass separating the entry from the office, they could clearly see the man whose family the Guardians had visited the other night as Olivia invited him to sit down in one of the chairs across from the desk.

"Thank you, kindly," the man said, his voice trailing into the living room through the open door. He sat, now holding his hat in his hands, looking very nervous.

"It'll just be a few minutes, Mr. Gusterson. Can I get you anything while you wait?"

"No, ma'am. I'll be just fine here. Thank you."

Olivia closed the blinds and shut the door before returning to them. She pulled out her phone, but before she could dial, it rang.

"He's here," she said quietly, but with a buzz of excitement. "Okay. Come in through the barn and we can go in together."

"And just what was all that about?" Penelope raised a brow.

"Matt Gusterson is a chef," Olivia said as if that explained everything. "Before he got married, he even trained at Le Chateaubriand in Paris."

The barn doors scraped against the floor as they opened.

"I'm beginning to see why we might need another entrance into the barn."

Everly perked up when Grayson walked through the door with Holden, Landon, Ian, and Owen laughing.

She had not expected him back until this afternoon. She set her cocoa on the end table next to the couch, beaming when he winked at her. She bit her lip.

"Sorry, Violet," Landon said with a chuckle. "I'm afraid your husband just met Brewster."

"I barely got away with my life," he said with an air of exasperation, and he flopped himself next to his wife on the couch and laid his cheek on her protruding belly.

Violet giggled, caressing his face.

"I have never seen a man's boots raise so high into the air when he runs."

Owen sat up.

"So, do we get to do it again tomorrow?" he asked hopefully.

Everyone laughed again.

Olivia grabbed Holden and Ian and they disappeared into the office, Landon joined Penelope on the floor, but Grayson didn't move. The late morning sunlight streamed through the open doors as the man she'd been introduced to after Sheila had been taken into custody as Mr. Hughes entered the barn. He wore a warm smile, so different from the expressions she'd seen on him yesterday as he'd followed her around. She still didn't understand why he hadn't just introduced himself and told her what was happening.

Everly moved her feet out from under her and stood up to greet him.

"Good morning, everyone," he said, removing the Gatsby hat he'd been wearing and stepped farther into the room. "Thank you for allowing me a few minutes of your time on this beautiful Christmas Eve morning. I'm headed back to Albuquerque in a bit, but needed to talk to you both before I do." He addressed Everly and Violet.

"Me?" her sister questioned.

"Come in and sit down, Mr. Hughes," Everly said, pointing to the empty oversized chair next to the couch.

He leaned forward, a little hesitant, but with a light push from Grayson, he conceded and walked toward them, flipping the back of his familiar dark overcoat up to sit down without restraint.

Grayson moved to her side, capturing her hand in his. She looked up at him.

"Hi," he said quietly with a wink.

"Hi," she returned, still relishing the warmth that spread through her every time he spoke.

Grayson sat down on the arm of the couch and encouraged her to retake her seat. She again folded her legs up on the cushions but leaned on him for support, then casually glanced over at the man sitting in the chair next to them.

"I never thought this day would come," he said, a hint of emotion in his voice. "You were both so little the last time I saw you in person." He set down the two-handled paper bag he'd been carrying on the floor next to his feet and then glanced up, peering from one sister to the other. "My name is Ward Hughes and I used to be involved with some very dangerous people." He cleared his throat, then looked up at Grayson. "This is harder than I thought it was going to be."

"Just tell them what you told me, and it will be fine."

Everly cranked her head upward and met Grayson's eyes. He squeezed her hand and nodded, offering her that beautiful assuring smile that told her everything would be all right.

"I knew your father."

Everly's heart sank. She didn't want to hear about her father, much less talk about him with a perfect stranger.

"He actually arrested me the night you were born, Everly," he said with a chuckle. "He was very good at his job," he added, almost wistfully.

"Because he cared more about being good at his job than being a good father."

"That's not true. In fact, he was very concerned that the job was taking him away from his family."

Everly scoffed.

"Ev," Violet said, reaching across her body and placing a hand on Everly's arm. "Let him speak."

"Over the course of several years, and after I'd done my time, something remarkable happened. Jason and I became friends. Good friends."

Everly could sense in him genuine sorrow as he spoke of their father. She knew that holding on to her anger was her way of protecting herself from the suffocating grief that would inevitably seep into her soul when she finally forgave him for leaving. For dying.

"I don't remember you."

"No, I'm not surprised. When you both were very young, we were celebrating Violet's fifth birthday in the backyard of your old house in Bridger Hills."

The thought triggered a brief memory of her mother and father blowing little plastic horns and laughing, both girls clutched playfully in their arms.

"An old mercenary team from my past crashed the party, putting your whole family at risk." He dropped his head. "It was just too dangerous for me to be around you girls after that, so, we decided it would be better for me to stay away for your protection and safety."

"I was playing over by the wishing well," Everly recalled, "and you scooped me up into your arms and hid me in the cab of our truck." She looked up at him. "And told me not to make a sound because we were playing a game of hide and seek."

"That's right," Hughes said, tears brimming the bottom lids of his eyes.

"I remember." With a brief glance at her sister, she placed her hand over Violet's on her arm.

Mr. Hughes swallowed hard. "Before your father died, he made me swear if anything ever happened to him, that I would watch over you from afar." He bent down and reached into the small sack he'd brought with him and retrieved two packages, handing the smaller of them to her and the larger one to Violet. "A box of his old things somehow made it to my house last week, so when Jacobi called and threatened me with information he'd collected years before, I saw it as an opportunity to finally deliver what should have already been yours.

The hairs on the back of Everly's neck bristled at the mention of her former boss.

"What's this?" she asked.

Hughes jutted his head forward, motioning for her to open it. Inside she discovered an old-fashioned pocket watch with a shield, an eagle, and a flag on the front that read, 'To Serve and Protect.'

Everly sucked in a breath. She recognized it immediately. It was the one she'd given her father when she was a child—antique silver, an eagle with a flag on a shield sitting in its center with legs extended—one clutching an olive branch and the other blades of wheat. A large heart sat at the bottom and the words 'TO SERVE AND PROTECT' were written in a circular pattern around the symbols.

"Where did you get this?" she asked in hushed tones, afraid her voice might crack with emotion. She clicked it open. There, tucked into the concave lid, sat an old, worn photograph of her and Violet as young girls, hugging and laughing together at a park.

Hughes spoke softly, his own voice filled with sentiment. "Your father carried this watch everywhere with him. He wanted to keep his daughters close to his heart no matter where he went. That photo," he pointed to the lid, "he placed there himself so he could see his two wonderful girls anytime he wanted."

The tears flowed freely now, streaming down her cheeks. She clutched it to her chest, overwhelmed by the tender thought.

"He was going to quit the force as soon as he finished his last case."

Everly's eyes, wet with emotion, shot up to meet his,

searching for the truth in their depths.

Hughes confirmed with a nod, and Everly's whole body shook with a sob.

Grayson slipped his arm around her, placed a light kiss on the top of her head, and handed her a tissue.

"And, Violet," he said, motioning to the worn and weathered leather-bound book she held, "this was your father's journal. He documented so many stories of you two growing up, of his regrets at not being there when you needed him, how proud he was of each of you."

Violet caressed the top of the journal with a trembling hand, her eyes moist as she unwrapped the single leather strap that kept it closed. She opened it, then turned it around for Everly to see—their father's distinct handwriting scratched on its pages.

"Your father was a great man. He knew you needed him, and he wanted to be there for you, but he was taken from you before he could make up for lost time."

Everly leaned over to wrap her arms around her sister.

"He didn't leave, Vi!"

"I know."

Grayson's phone rang.

"Sorry." He looked down at Everly apologetically. "Excuse me a moment," he said, holding up one finger as he moved into the kitchen.

Hughes stood up.

"Thank you, Mr. Hughes," Violet said, standing up with the help of a little push from Owen. "This means the world to us."

Everly followed suit. "Yes, thank you! We had no idea our dad had someone looking out for us."

Mr. Hughes smiled, a warm, father-like smile that erased any lingering doubt. "You know that drive that has been the cause of all this mess?" he asked.

Everly nodded.

"It contains records of the evidence your father was attempting to retrieve the night he was killed."

"What does that mean, Mr. Hughes."

"YES!" Grayson shouted from the kitchen and came running into the room. He nodded at Hughes, visibly itching to deliver some information.

"That means his killer has been identified."

Everly's browns scrunched together. "But he died in an accident."

"A high-speed chase," Violet added.

"Yes, when a large vehicle struck him broadside."

"Peter Jacobi was arrested just fifteen minutes ago."

"Jacobi killed my father?" Everly's eyes shifted between Hughes and Grayson.

Both confirmed with a nod.

"And now, because of you, he'll be going to prison for a very, very long time."

She rushed into Grayson's arms.

"I'd still like to check in on you girls from time to time if that's all right with you. I hope that any danger from my past is long behind me, but it does bring me comfort that you'll have Sheriff Kane around to keep you safe."

Grayson squeezed her tighter.

"Please don't be a stranger," Everly said, slipping from Grayson's arms and hugging the older man.

Violet joined them.

She placed a light kiss on the man's cheek.

"Thank you."

The office door opened into the entryway. Holden, Olivia, Mr. Gusterson, and Ian all filed out. Everyone turned to look at them.

"Okay," Olivia said, her brow raised, her head cocked, and her hands on her hips. "What did we miss?"

Everly glanced around the room. Penelope was tucked under Landon's arm, wiping tears from her face. Grayson stood with a grin from ear to ear, Owen now stood in front of the couch, and she and her sister were still hugging Mr. Hughes. A giggle burst from her lips that was highly unexpected, and before long, everyone was laughing.

"Don't worry, Liv," Everly said, leaning forward, her arm still around Mr. Hughes, "I'll fill you in later."

With one last squeeze, Mr. Hughes took in a deep breath. "While I could get used to this, I've got quite a long drive ahead of me, so I best get going."

For the first time since Everly was a little girl, she felt close to her father having his friend here with them and knowing he'd been watching out for them for the better part of their lives.

"Won't you stay?" she asked.

"Unless you need to get home to your eighty-seven-year-old mother and cat named Fred," Grayson said earnestly.

Everly's brows crumpled together.

That was oddly specific.

"Mama passed just over a year ago now," Hughes said. "And Fred hasn't been with us in a good long while." He laughed knowingly. "But I understand that the inn is full."

He was right. Violet and Owen only had a one-night reservation for last night and were originally going to be heading home tonight, but when Grayson called them, he'd invited them to stay in the barn over Christmas with Everly, so they'd made the necessary arrangements to stay.

"Well, I have it on good authority," Grayson said as he sat down on the couch, his feet extended and his hands folded behind his head, "that one Sheila Reed will not be needing her reservation for tonight. I could make a call if it would be helpful." His dimpled grin made Everly's heart flutter.

"I accept."

"Everly, might we speak with you for a moment?" Olivia asked.

"That didn't go so well for me last time," she said with

only a tinge of reservation. She glanced over at Grayson who simply winked at her, his smile reflecting a hint of mischievousness.

"No interrogations or accusations to follow," Olivia promised.

"Join us tonight at the tree-lighting?" Everly asked Mr. Hughes before leaving.

"I can't think of anywhere I would rather be."

"This is Matt Gusterson," Olivia said, introducing them as they all walked back into her office.

"I'm looking forward to working with you, Miss Quinn." The man extended his hand. "Now, if you'll all excuse me, I have another Christmas miracle to share. See you early next week to experiment with some of my recipes?"

"Yes, Matt," Olivia piped in. "Take a few days to enjoy some time with your wife and kids. We'll see you on Wednesday."

Everly wasn't sure what was happening, so she just smiled awkwardly and waved.

"What exactly just happened?" she asked, turning around and glancing over the three faces staring hopefully at her.

"Everly?"

"Olivia?"

"We know you've had a lot to process in a very short time—with Grayson, your ex, that publicist who threatened to kill you, the accident—"

"Liv," Holden slipped his arm around his wife and placed a kiss on her temple.

"...and we want to be sensitive to that, but we..." She hesitated, shaking her hands, more nervous or maybe more excited than Everly had yet to see. It was difficult to tell if she was pausing for dramatic effect or because she wasn't sure how to say whatever it was she wanted to say.

Then, in a rush of spilled words, Olivia said, "We want you to be the Creative Director and Operations Manager of

The Barn at Blackwood Ranch and stay right here in the barn—to develop design concepts, media campaigns, and basically run the whole show—with the help of Matt as your executive chef, and a new team of your choosing."

"Wait, let's back up the truck a little." She took a deep breath. "You want to offer me a job? Here at Silver Springs?"

"Well, technically, it would be here at The Barn at Blackwood Ranch, but—"

"Yes! I accept," Everly squealed, delighted at the prospect of staying close to the people she'd already grown to love so much over the last few days.

Lists started pouring into her mind, ideas swirled around in her head, and she started making a mental note of everything that would need to be done in a relatively short time.

STOP! she commanded her mind to quiet. There would be plenty of time to figure out the logistics. For now, it just felt right and that was all she needed to know.

"Don't you even want to know what we can offer you?"

"Is it fair?"

"Yes."

"Does it mean I get to stay here with all of you?"

"Yes."

"Will it utilize my skills and talents?"

"Yes!"

"Then, I accept."

CHAPTER SEVENTEEN

Grayson had handed Sheila off to the U.S. Marshals earlier than expected today. For once, they'd not left him hanging until the last hours of the night. He guessed they were just as keen on getting home to be with their families on Christmas Eve as he was.

He'd called around to several shops and discovered several that would still be open for a few more hours before closing up for the holidays. He grabbed his coat from the rack beside the door and headed out into the refreshingly clear afternoon.

"I didn't realize you were seeing anyone, Sheriff," Mr. Rothman said as Grayson perused the rings in his ample display.

"It's fairly recent. But when you know…"

"You know. I've heard that once or twice before," the jeweler said with a knowing smile. "Do you have any idea what you might be looking for?"

"I think I'll just know it when I see it."

After shopping three other jewelers already, discouragement began to set in as he could not find anything that spoke to him.

"Thanks anyway, Mr. Rothman," he told the shorter, greying gentleman behind the counter.

Everly deserved the best and he needed to find one that would be both beautiful and unique—just like her.

In a small town like Silver Falls, there were a limited number of choices, but that didn't deter him. He was determined to get what he needed and in time for the tree-lighting tonight, and if that meant a quick trip into Boulder, then he might have to the brave the canyon.

After nearly two more hours of searching, he'd still come up empty, and it occurred to him that all he needed for tonight was something simple and original. A promise ring of sorts, though, he argued with himself, he would marry her tomorrow if she'd allow it. His heart nearly skipped a beat as he entertained that thought.

He'd seen a few silversmiths at the festival and most of their pieces were handcrafted and unique. If he headed over that direction, he had no doubts that he'd be able to find what he was looking for, then they could go together to pick out something a little brag-worthy.

When Grayson pulled up into the east parking lot, his chest tightened at the site of Sheila's big truck still sitting where they'd left it last night. He pulled out his phone, but before he could dial Gertrude, she pulled up behind him. The vehicle would have to be processed and all evidence packed up and sent back to New Mexico, but not today. If they were lucky, the prosecuting office would request to have the truck processed locally and they would come pick it up.

"Thanks, Gertie," he called out to the woman before heading down to the square. "Merry Christmas."

It didn't take long before he found Everly. She stood at the front of the reindeer corral, feeding one of the harnessed animals and handing out food to children and other festivalgoers to do the same. She looked radiant, her eyes sparkling with holiday cheer. He made his way over to her, pausing at her side and leaning in.

"Hello, beautiful," he greeted with a grin.

Everly turned, her eyes widening in surprise.

"Well, hello yourself, handsome," she said, giggling as the reindeer finished eating the Christmas mixture of oats and bits of apple from her palm.

"They seem to like you." He slipped his arms around her, his cheek resting against the side of her head.

"I like them." She spun in his arms to face him. "Have you seen your granddad's paintings? He has some really beautiful portraits of Agnes."

"Agnes? Who's Agnes?"

"She's the reindeer that comes to visit the veranda on the back of the barn."

Grayson laughed out loud. "You're naming the reindeer now?"

"Yep."

"Do you have any idea how attractive you are to me right now?"

"Because I started naming reindeer?"

"Uh, huh," he said, lowering his head toward her. "Tell me another."

She giggled.

"Edith."

He dipped lower.

"Ethyl."

He was now only a breath away from capturing her lips with his.

"Winifred."

He laughed, resting his forehead against hers. "Winifred? Why not Winnie or Freddie or just Wynn for short?"

"Hey, mister," a child's voice called out, "will you stop trying to distract the lady so she can get us some food for the reindeer, please?"

Everly laughed.

He stole a quick kiss, then backed away so she could do the job he guessed his mother had assigned her.

"See you around, Albuquerque," he said with a smile and a little spring in his step.

"I'll be heading over to your booth next," she called out after him.

He could only imagine how his mother had had her running from one place to another all afternoon and he chuckled to himself. She certainly fit right into the family, and he couldn't wait to make it official.

There were only three silver artisans today with rings on display. Several unique pieces stood out to him, but none that seemed quite fitting for his proposal. Thick coiled bands, rings with baubled ends, and pieces with large turquoise or onyx stones made up a huge part of the original inventory in the first two booths, and while they were beautiful and unique to be sure, Grayson felt the prick of disappointment that nothing seemed just right in his otherwise hopeful search.

With only one booth left, he offered a quick prayer for a sprig of Christmas magic to find its way to him.

"Hey, kid," his granddad called as he passed. The older man carefully wrapped his paintings before setting them upright in wooden cases he'd built to contain and transport his artwork.

"Do you need some help, Granddad?" Grayson asked.

"Nope."

"Glad to see you made it in time for the tree-lighting."

Grayson sat down on the stool at the front of his booth and took a moment to appreciate his granddad's talent.

"You did do a great job at capturing Agnes," Grayson said appreciatively.

"You've been talking to that sweet gal of yours."

"How did you know?" Granddad chuckled. "Did you find what you were looking for?"

"'Fraid not."

"I hoped you might say that."

"Granddad?"

The family patriarch pulled a deep emerald velvet pouch from the interior pocket of his fur-lined denim coat and placed it in Grayson's hand.

"I had an inkling that you might need it tonight."

Grayson tipped the bag until its contents spilled out onto his palm.

A ring.

He had never seen anything of its kind. Two thin strands of silver, meticulously crafted to mimic twig vines intertwined merging at the base of an exquisite cushion diamond in its center with small diamonds strategically placed like flower blooms along the base. And a wedding band to match.

"Your grandmother's ring is unique and rare as Everly. You are looking to propose tonight, aren't you?"

"How did you know?"

"I imagine I had the same look in my eye when I proposed to my Maggie—just five days after we met, by the way. At the Christmas Eve tree-lighting ceremony just over fifty years ago on this very square."

"Really? How did I not know that before?" Grayson asked, grateful he shared some of his granddad's romantic spirit. "It's perfect, Granddad. Just perfect."

"By the way, son, the sleigh'll be parked over behind the gazebo." He held up his hand before Grayson could even ask the questions. "Have I never taught you not to look a gift horse in the mouth?"

"Yes, sir."

"Behind the gazebo. Got it." He slipped the rings back into the bag and tucked it safely into his pocket. "And Granddad…"

"Hmmm?"

"Thank you!"

The sun was starting to fade and many of the artisans had

already begun cleaning up and putting away their wares so they would be ready for the tree-lighting ceremony. Grayson glanced down at his watch.

Less than an hour to go. He reminded himself to breathe when he rounded the corner on his patrol to see Everly at the hot cocoa station, sheer joy on her face as she chatted with customers and handed them steaming cups of cocoa. He liked to think that he had a little something to do with the glow that now touched her cheeks.

With a playful grin, he approached the booth, the heady aroma of chocolate and peppermint filling the air.

"Why, Sheriff, it's so good of you to support such a wonderful cause this evening. What can I get you?"

"How about a date to the tree-lighting tonight?"

"Hmmm, I don't know what comes in that one. A little sugar, maybe? A little spice?"

"And everything nice," he smiled, then leaned over the counter for a quick kiss.

"That's what dates with me are made of," she whispered.

"Arggg...can the two of you be any gooier?" Penelope's voice held a hint of teasing.

"Why, yes, ma'am, I do believe we could," he said with one more quick kiss before backing away. He glanced over and winked at his sister-in-law, who chuckled with a slight shake of her head.

"Your mama's looking for you. One of your art pieces is a little too heavy for her to load into the wagon."

"On it." He turned back to Everly. "Pick you up in twenty minutes?"

"I'll be waiting."

"Okay, Everly," Penelope said as she leaned down onto the counter, "that man has always been a little playful and a lot charming, but I have never seen him so...so..."

"Twitterpated?" Landon offered as he came up behind his wife and slipped his arms around her.

"That's not twitterpated, little brother," Holden said also joining them, Olivia by his side, holding his hand.

"That's love," she said knowingly.

Heat rose in Everly's cheeks, her heart fuller than she had ever experienced before as she glanced out over the people who had so quickly moved in to occupy the empty spaces of her life. She loved him too—loved all of them.

Another volunteer came to relieve Everly of her hot cocoa station responsibilities, so she exited through the little shop door and joined the others.

"Can I let you all in on a little secret? I've never actually been to a tree-lighting before. I only know what I've seen in the movies, and even then, it seems like it's just a bunch of people standing around a large tree waiting for some special person to flip a switch and turn on the big tree's lights."

"Yep, that about covers it," Landon said matter-of-factly.

Penelope tapped his chest playfully.

"Nonsense," Cass said, she and Ben appearing out of nowhere. "The Silver Falls Tree-Lighting is one of the town's most time-honored traditions at Christmas. My parents were engaged right here under that very tree."

"You mean, it's a real tree?"

"Of course, it's a real tree," Holden teased. "Colorado's full of them."

"I mean, it's planted in the town square, alive, growing?"

"Yes. Isn't it beautiful?"

"Ho! Ho! Ho!" The booming voice bearing Santa's call rang through the air as squeals from delighted children converged on the sleigh pulled by no less than eight beautiful reindeer decked out in red tack and jingle bells.

Everly almost felt like a child again as she watched the excitement of the festivalgoers as they waited within the cordoned off area for Santa to pass by. She giggled at the sight of Grayson, Wesley, and Deputy Gonzalez working as elves, handing out presents and treats to all the children whose eyes were wide, alight with anticipation and so full of the Christmas spirit.

As she looked through the small crowd, she saw Matt Gusterson and his little family trying to see Santa, but there were just too many people for them to reach the front. One child, she guessed the youngest of the two, sat on her father's shoulders as he held the other—no more than four—in his arm. The youngster moved from one side to the other in the hopes of seeing Santa. Without a thought, Everly walked up next to Matt and nudged him.

"Do you mind if I help?" she asked, motioning to the young boy in his arms.

"Miss Quinn?" he said with some surprise, placing a hand in the small of his wife's back. "Ava, this is Miss Quinn, my new boss."

"Everly, please," she said with a smile. "It's very nice to meet you, Ava. And who do we have here?" she asked, her eyes flitting between the children.

"This is Cooper," Matt said said, indicating the boy he held, "and this little munchkin," he wiggled the foot of the toddler sitting on his own shoulders, "is Eleanor."

"Hello. My name is—"

"Everly," Cooper said with confidence, and she beamed at the child.

"Yes, it is. Cooper, would you like to crawl up onto my shoulders like your sister for a better look at Santa? I know him, you know."

The boy glanced up at his father, who nodded.

"Yes, please!" he said heartily, already leaning out of his father's arms into Everly's. "Can we meet him? Can we meet Santa?"

"Tonight is a very busy night for the big guy, you know, but we can try."

Cooper nodded.

She'd expected the child to weigh a lot more than he did, and found the increased burden on her shoulders light as she made her way through the crowd. When she reached a place at the front toward the end of the line where she wouldn't worry about the boy blocking any other children behind them, Cooper wiggled, and she imagined him to be waving at Santa as the sleigh finally passed before them, and she smiled.

It only took a moment for Grayson to spot them, and she was rewarded with a dimpled grin that spread wide across his ridiculously handsome face. They continued to hand out gifts until the big red velvety sack in the back compartment of the sleigh was nearly depleted.

Matt, Ava, and Eleanor joined them just as Santa reached the end of his gift-giving route.

Wes handed Eleanor a package with bright red and green polka dots that Everly knew was a beautiful new doll with long blond curls just like the girl's, and Grayson held out a Christmas-striped box for the boy.

"Nah, I don't need nothin' more, thanks," Cooper said seriously. "I just wanna speak to the big guy."

Everly bit her lip at the use of her own words to describe Santa earlier.

Obviously, surprised, Grayson nodded appreciatively. "I think that can be arranged." He popped open the gate and allowed Everly inside the designated route area.

She walked up to where Ian now sat, perched on the bench seat.

"Is that Cooper Gusterson you have there, Miss Quinn?" Ian asked, the small, round spectacles he wore sitting perfectly at the tip of his nose.

"Why, yes, Santa. This young man desired an audience.'

"I love you, Santa," Cooper said, flinging himself from her shoulders and into the sleigh where Ian played his role flawlessly. The little boy threw his arms around Santa's neck and closed his eyes. "Oh, thank you for helping God make Mommy and Daddy happy again for Christmas."

Her throat constricted, knowing to what the boy referred, and she was humbled she'd been witness to such an innocent plea of gratitude.

It also took a moment before Ian could respond, his eyes wet and his jaw clenched.

"You're a good boy, young Gusterson," he finally managed, then cleared his throat. "I'm glad that you already understand what, no, who this season is all about."

"Yes, sir. The baby Jesus," he said proudly.

"That's right." Ian slipped a small trinket into the boy's hand with a wink. "Merry Christmas," he said, then followed with a loud, "Ho! Ho! Ho!"

Cooper jumped back into Everly's arms as Santa urged the reindeer forward. In minutes, he had disappeared around the corner of Santa's Village.

The boy opened his hand to reveal an antique-looking coin. "What does it say?" he asked, holding it up to her.

"Let's see. It says, 'Official Bearer of the Christmas Spirit." She turned it over. "Share the Joy."

"What do you got there, buddy?" Matt asked.

Everly set him down on the ground and the little boy ran over to his father, proudly holding up his coin.

"Sheriff," Matt said, holding out a hand. "The gratitude we have for what your family has done for us this season cannot be overstated. I know he's very busy tonight, but will you thank *Santa* again for saving our home? After I lost my job, bills started piling up and we were at our wits end trying to figure out how to make everything work, and with Christmas and the baby coming, we were in need of nothing short of a miracle. And we've received several. I still can't believe Ian bought the mortgage on our home and started us out current. And with the new job at The Barn…" he got a little choked up.

Everly knew she should be shocked by the revelation that
Ian had both the resources and the influence to pull off such a
feat in such a short time, but somehow it rang true for him.
Ian Redbourne was a good man.

And, she looked over at the sheriff, *so is his grandson.*

Grayson slipped his arm around Everly so naturally it was
as if he'd done it a thousand times before. She smiled and
returned her gaze to the young family.

"Please just tell him how grateful we are," Ava said,
placing a hand on her husband's arm. "His generosity and
Olivia's have given us a fresh start and we'll never forget it.
Oooo," she winced rubbing her belly. "He's a kicker, this
one," she said with a laugh.

"When are you due?" Everly asked.

"Forty-eight days," the woman was quick to respond.

Everly laughed. "My sister is due next week. The two of
you should commiserate."

"Come on, you two," Grayson's dad called as he passed
by them, headed quickly toward the giant town Christmas tree,
a large battery in tow. "Your Christmas wishes aren't going to
write themselves."

Christmas wishes?

"It's good to see you, Matt," Grayson said, "but now if
you'll excuse us."

"Oh, yes, of course."

"Merry Christmas," Everly said with a smile. "We'll see
you next week. Wednesday, right?"

"Yes, ma'am. I'll be there. Merry Christmas."

Grayson took her by the hand and led her over to the tree.
A large craft table had been set up, cluttered with green, red,
and white round ornament-style tags, dozens of markers and
pens, and glitter for decorating their wishes.

"How is this supposed to work exactly?" Everly asked,
picking up one of the paper ornaments.

"The idea is to write the wish that is dearest to your heart this Christmas and for the year to come. Tradition has it that the more wishes hung on the tree—wishes of joy, peace, and love rather than selfish desires, mind you—when the lights are illuminated on the tree, the likelihood of our wishes being fulfilled is increased.

"And what did you wish for last year, Sheriff Kane?" Everly asked playfully.

"Don't tell anyone," he said, "but I've never actually hung an ornament on the tree."

This news surprised her.

"So, why this year?"

"Because I have more hope than ever that my wishes will come true this Christmas."

"Good answer," she said, leaning into him, relishing the mere touch of him.

They hung their ornaments on the tree, and stood back, waiting for the mayor to begin the ceremony. Eli and Rachel moved up to the front to stand next to the podium. Everly hadn't seen either one of them today, but it made sense that the town council would have invited the famous author of their own little children's book to be the guest to light the tree.

Grayson's dad knelt on the ground, next to the battery he'd carried in earlier, tools in hand, and a bead of sweat touching his brow.

After a few brief words from the mayor, Eli stood up, thanked everyone for their hospitality—to his credit, avoiding any mention of yesterday's incident—then, grabbed the handle of the power switch.

An apprehensive and worried smile stretched over Ben Kane's face, one eye partially closed.

And on. Eli shifted the switch upward and all the lights on the tree illuminated.

Ben blew out a relieved breath, his smile now genuine as he pulled himself up to his feet and slipped an arm around his grinning wife.

Everly laughed.

A band played familiar Christmas songs from the gazebo and the crowd began to sing along.

"Come with me," Grayson said, again scooping her hand in his.

"Where are we going?" she asked, giggling.

He pulled her around the back of the gazebo where the Belgians had been hitched to their however many great granddaddy's sleigh.

Santa sat in the driver's seat. Ian looked over his shoulder and winked at her.

Several very cozy-looking blankets had been laid out in the back.

"There doesn't seem to be a cloud in the sky tonight, and I thought you might want to go for a ride with me and gaze at the stars."

"How very romantic of you."

"It is, isn't it? I get that from my granddaddy," he said with a smile, a fleeting glance up at Santa as he held out a hand to help her up, then swept across the air in front of him with the other.

She climbed up into the back of the sleigh, surprised at the comfort of the seats. The blankets were similar to those Olivia had all throughout the barn and Everly pulled one up around her.

Grayson followed her in, and sat down next to her, fighting with one of the blankets to get his feet beneath it.

"Oh, Sheriff," a high-pitched sing-song voice called from behind them.

Grayson breathed a heavy sigh but quickly replaced his exasperation with a smile and leaned forward to greet the woman.

"Finally," the brazen redhead said breathily, peering inside, obviously surprised to see that the sheriff was not alone. "You are a hard person to track down, Grayson Kane."

Everly offered a small wave.

Almost as if not knowing what to do about Everly, the woman set the town calendar down awkwardly on Grayson's lap, already opened to December, and handed him a marker. "Sign it for me? Pretty please?" she asked, her voice laced with syrupy undertones.

Everly could swear that she'd batted her eyelashes at him. With a few flicks of his wrist, he etched out his name.

"You are nothing if not persistent, Shelby," Grayson said, handing the marker back to her. "I'll give you that. Sorry that I wasn't available when you dropped by the house before. I trust you're doing well?"

The woman glanced over the page with his signature across the bottom of his picture.

"Aren't you going to add a personal note to me, Sheriff?" she asked, holding out the marker for him again. "We've known each other an awfully long time, after all."

"Sure, Shelby," he said with a good-natured chortle, taking the marker from her and scribbling a short message above his name.

"And, yes, I am doing well, thank you for asking," she added as she waited.

Once he finished her inscription, she took a moment to read over it right there.

"Why if that isn't the sweetest thing, Sheriff," she cooed with a satisfied grin. "I hope you have a very merry Christmas," she said with a wave. Then, as she turned to leave, she glanced back over her shoulder. "Merry Christmas to you too, Sheriff's friend."

"Everly," she provided.

Shelby nodded curtly, then turned before practically skipping away.

"You too, Shelby," he called after her with a wave and a genuine smile, chuckle, and light shake of his head.

Without any delay, the sleigh started moving and in

moments, it was like they had traveled through a door into an entirely different world. A different time. Unlike the first couple of nights she'd been there, the skies were clear. The moon shone over wide open fields, lit up the snowcapped mountaintops, and offered her a view of the handsome man's features next to her.

"Why Sheriff Grayson Kane, I do believe this entire town is in love with you," Everly stated playfully as a light breeze caused her to snuggle into him a little closer, pulling the blanket up around her neck.

He turned to face her, the playful glint in his eyes vanishing as he gently slid his arm around her, drawing her close, the warmth of him a magnet to her chilled frame.

"Maybe," his unassuming acknowledgment not a sign of arrogance, but acceptance. "However, the only question that matters, the one that presses on my mind, is whether or not the woman who holds the whole of my heart in her hands, is in love with me too."

Everly tilted her chin upward and stared up at him, his words like something Blakely Blackwood might say in one of Olivia's novels.

Grayson smiled uncomfortably. "What is it that that Mr. Darcy said?" He took a deep breath. "You are too generous to trifle with me." His voice was low, resonant, earnest. "Do you love me?" He waited, patiently, expectantly.

Who was this man? Was he for real?

The butterflies returned to Everly's chest, a giddy feeling bubbling up from somewhere inside of her.

"You know Jane Austen?" she asked with a breathy laugh.

"Everly?" his voice was a plea.

"Yes, Grayson, sweetheart, darling, you *are* the love of my life." She slipped a hand out of the blanket and rested it on his face. "I am yours. Wholeheartedly yours."

"Marry me," he said without any hesitation. He felt around for something in his pocket, and suddenly, there, between his thumb and forefinger, he held a diamond ring. It was impossible to see the details in this light, but it didn't matter. He could have torn the ring from a soda bottle and her answer would have been the same.

"Anytime. Anywhere."

He slipped the ring onto her finger, then wrapped his warm hand around her freezing one. He leaned down, his head tilted, his mouth so close to hers. Everly's pulse quickened in expectation.

"I love you, Albuquerque," he whispered, his lips parted ever so slightly as they claimed hers in a kiss that promised forever.

CHAPTER EIGHTEEN

Everly had awoken in the early morning hours, unable to sleep for excitement. After throwing on her coat and sitting outside on her veranda for several minutes expressing all her excitement, obstacles, plans, and worries with Agnes in the frigid air, she'd crawled back under her heavenly blankets to lie on her heavenly pillow and had fallen back to sleep.

COCK-A-DOODLE-DOO.

She'd heard about Brewster the rooster, but this was the first morning, she'd actually heard him crow.

Rays from the morning sun spilled in through the bedroom windows, bursting outward from just above the mountain peaks in her current view. Flecks of light danced on the walls above the wood-framed double doors leading out to the veranda. It took a moment before she realized the little spectacles were coming from the light reflecting off the diamonds in her ring.

She glanced down at the intricate silver pattern, and couldn't stop admiring the complete uniqueness that now adorned her finger. It was exquisite, beyond anything she could have hoped for.

Grayson had informed her that it had belonged to his grandmother, and that had endeared it to her even more than she could have possibly imagined.

Knock. Knock.

Reluctantly, Everly threw back her blankets and rolled out of her cozy bed, slipped her feet into her cute little fuzzy animal slippers, and traipsed over to her bedroom door, swinging it open without a thought.

"Good morning, my beautiful bride-to-be," Grayson said, leaning in and giving her a light kiss, chuckling softly as he glanced up at her hair. "Sleep well?"

"What are you doing here so early?" she asked, quickly running a hand over her hair in an attempt to tame even a few of the whispies that were sure to be there.

"Let me see that hand of yours," he said, leaning up against the doorframe. She held it up in front of her to admire it once again before bringing it up to rest momentarily over her heart to display.

"Do you have any idea how happy you have made me, Grayson Kane?" she said with a smile. She didn't know why she liked saying his full name.

Is that his full name?

It was odd to think she didn't know.

He grabbed her by the waist and pulled her in closer. "Tell me."

"Blissfully so," she told him, standing on her tiptoes to give him another kiss. "Do you have a middle name?" she asked so it wouldn't occupy her brain all morning.

"Taggart," he said with an affirmative nod. "After my Uncle Tag."

"Grayson Taggart Kane. It's just perfect."

"And you? Any middle names or maiden names I should know about?" he asked, the playful grin on his face showing off his dimples.

"Nope. No middle name. And no past husbands to speak of I'm afraid. Just plain old Everly Quinn."

"It's perfect," he replied.

There was still so much they didn't know about each other, but that they would have a lifetime to discover. That thought pleased her beyond all reason.

"You are so beautiful," he said with awe.

Heat crept into her face and she pushed away from him.

"Do you just wake up looking that perfect every morning?" she asked, lightly appalled at the thought. She raised a brow and pulled her lip in between her teeth as she glanced over him—blue, grey, and white plaid pajama bottoms topped with a heathered Henley tee. "That," she put her palm out toward him and rotated it in circles, "is a good look for you."

She could have sworn his cheeks darkened a shade under her appraisal.

He tilted his head and shrugged his shoulder. "I've been up for a little while now, but you…" he grabbed her by the hand and pulled her back into his embrace.

She bit her lip again.

"Woman, I'm telling you, you've got to stop doing that or you will be the end of me."

"What?" she asked, not quite sure to what he was referring, but liking his response to it.

He didn't say anything for a long moment, but he raised a brow, and a knowing smile touched his lips.

"All right, come on," he said, letting her go, taking a step backward, and clapping his hands together. "Everyone is waiting."

"And when you say everyone," she narrowed her eyes at him, "you mean…"

"Everyone," he confirmed. "Santa decided to drop all of our presents in the barn this year and stay for breakfast."

"Okay." She took a deep breath.

"And no changing," he said. "We're all in our Christmas pajamas."

"Give me five minutes to brush my teeth and do something with this mop."

"I think you look sexy just like that," he said with an appraising grin and raise to his brow.

"Five minutes."

He nodded and turned to leave, then paused, leaning back into the room.

"Merry Christmas."

"Merry Christmas, Grayson."

Less than five minutes later, she pinched her cheeks before walking out into the living room—overcome with a wave of emotion at the sight that greeted her. It had been just Violet and her for so many years, and then for the last several, after Vi and Owen had gotten married and moved up here to Colorado, she'd spent Christmas alone. To see so many faces she loved and who loved her in return touched her heart deeply.

Don't cry. Don't cry. Don't cry.

"We probably should have warned you that we are all like children on Christmas morning and get up even before that blasted rooster of Daddy's." Cass was the first to stand and greet her. "Good morning, sweetheart," she said with a kiss on her cheek. "Merry Christmas."

"Merry Christmas."

She and Grayson had decided to wait to tell anyone about the engagement until this morning as a Christmas surprise. They'd sworn Ian to secrecy, but one look at Grayson and his affirming nod, she couldn't wait to share the news.

The room fell silent, and everyone stared up at her expectantly.

"What?" she asked. "Do I have something on my face?" She reached up to brush her cheeks with her hand and the room erupted in squeals and laughter. The women all jumped up and fell all over her, and the men turned to Grayson, shaking his hand, then pulling him into big bear hugs.

After they'd eaten breakfast, everyone gathered out by the fire. A blanket of Christmas presents sat beneath the tree, stockings hung on the fireplace, and festive music played overhead.

Grateful she'd had a moment to wrap the only gift she'd purchased for Grayson at one of the festival booths, she'd taken a moment to slip it beneath the tree last night before she'd finally retired to bed.

She caught Violet's eye, and her sister beamed at her.

"I love you," she mouthed.

"I love you back," Everly mouthed in return.

Granddad sat at the foot of the tree and one by one, he passed out the gifts. Everly sat down in front of Grayson and leaned back against him, his arm and shoulder holding her possessively close to him as he supported himself on one hand with his legs extended in front of the couch where Violet and Owen snuggled together.

Everly couldn't help but laugh when she opened a brand-new pillow, all her own, just like those the barn would offer its guests, but when she opened the envelope on the tree with her name on it, she stared at the contents, wide-eyed and disbelieving.

"I want you to take me to that little café in San Sebastian with the Spanish food thingys that you love so much. I thought maybe we could go for our honeymoon."

"But these tickets are booked only a month from now."

"'Anytime. Anywhere,'" he quoted her words back to her. "I know what I want, Everly. 'And I never wish to be parted from you from this day on.'"

"Is he quoting Jane Austen?" Violet asked in a whisper.

Everly nodded.

"Marry him, Everly."

"I am."

Grayson smiled. "If I could marry you today, I would."

She waited for a familiar pit to form in her stomach, but it didn't come. Instead, she was filled with a belief in a love that she didn't know existed. She searched his eyes, for what she was unsure. All she did know was that she couldn't walk away from him, not now, not ever.

He was her home. He was her everything.

"I will." Even as she said the words, she knew they were true, and she quieted all the parts of her mind screaming for plans and preparations and details.

It'll keep.

When Everly's gift for Grayson was the last thing beneath the tree, Ian handed it to her.

Everly turned around to face him, her legs crossed in front of her. She handed him the small, buffalo-check-wrapped box.

After he tore the wrapping from the box and opened the lid, his eyes gained an amused glint as he fingered the material of the deep red scarf she had chosen for him.

"I think it will look great under your shearling coat," she praised.

When he pulled the scarf from the box, her father's pocket watch fell out into his hand.

"I know it's not a life-changing pillow or a trip to Spain…"

Grayson's jaw clenched, and he swallowed hard, shaking his head with checked emotion.

He clicked open the antique setting, and there, where the picture of her and Violet used to be, was now the selfie Everly and Grayson had taken in front of the sleigh. Penelope had helped her get it sized and printed.

It was a moment before he could speak, but he met her eyes, grabbing her folded legs and pulling her as close to him as he could. Then, he reached up, tucking a stray strand of hair behind her ear, and moved his hand to the side of her face.

"This," he started with a marked catch in his voice. Then

he cleared his throat. "I will always be present for you, Everly. And I will let you know today and remind you every day for the rest of our lives, that no scarf or pillow, trip or watch will ever compare to the gift that is you. You, Everly, sweetheart, darling, love of my life, are the greatest gift."

If you enjoyed Grayson and Everly's story, please take a few moments to return to the Grayson's Gift product page and leave a review now while it's still fresh in your mind. They are very appreciated, and every single one helps draw more readers to books they might also like.

Just scroll down to the Customer Review section with the stars and immediately below the "Review this product" section, click the box that reads, "Write a customer review."

Thank you in advance!

REDBOURNE FAMILY TREE
HISTORICAL

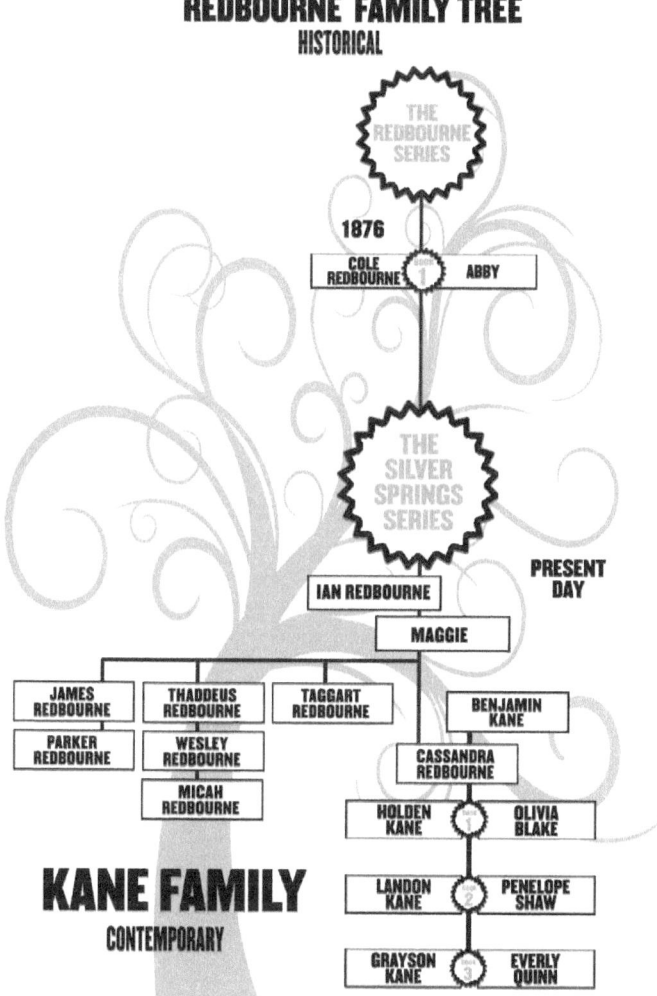

THE REDBOURNE SERIES

1876

COLE REDBOURNE — BOOK 1 — ABBY

THE SILVER SPRINGS SERIES

PRESENT DAY

IAN REDBOURNE

MAGGIE

JAMES REDBOURNE

THADDEUS REDBOURNE

TAGGART REDBOURNE

BENJAMIN KANE

PARKER REDBOURNE

WESLEY REDBOURNE

CASSANDRA REDBOURNE

MICAH REDBOURNE

HOLDEN KANE — BOOK 1 — OLIVIA BLAKE

KANE FAMILY
CONTEMPORARY

LANDON KANE — BOOK 2 — PENELOPE SHAW

GRAYSON KANE — BOOK 3 — EVERLY QUINN

ABOUT THE AUTHOR

KELLI ANN MORGAN is the international bestselling author of the beloved Redbourne Series, Deardon Mini-Series, and the Silver Springs Series. She writes inspirational romances with handsome, chivalrous men, strong, intelligent women, and a host of other characters that will feel like family. Her novels are highly romantic, full of action, and always leave you with a happily-ever-after. She lives in northern Utah near the beautiful mountains with her cute little family where she writes, runs her graphic design business, and enjoys many creative and artistic hobbies.

If you would like to receive new release alerts from Kelli Ann, please visit her website at http://www.kelliannmorgan.com where you can sign up for her newsletter.

FACEBOOK:
https://www.facebook.com/KelliAnnMorganAuthor

E-MAIL:
kelliann@kelliannmorgan.com

NEWSLETTER SIGN UP:
https://bit.ly/3pKJplE

.

www.ingramcontent.com/pod-product-compliance
Lightning Source LLC
Chambersburg PA
CBHW020327200626
46814CB00006BB/2453